A Mother Ru

by

Carolyn Walker

(with questions from a curious son)

Plain View Press
P. O. 33311
Austin, TX 78764

plainviewpress.com
sbright1@austin.rr.com
1-800-878-3605

Acknowledgments

I would like to express my gratitude to the following people who encouraged and helped me in this project:

Deb Woods
Kathy Garwood
Joe Sanders
Georgene Sloan
Myroslava Stefaniuk
Don Walker

Cover Art:

Christian Walker

Photograph of Author:

Gary Malerba

Most of these stories appeared in different forms in various newspapers.

Contents

The Pearl 7

Everyboy 9

Busted Things   11

A Mother's Faith   13

Realities   15

Mrs. X Has a Religious Experience   17

An Old Mother's Tale   20

Bewitched 22

A Halloween Surprise   24

Mrs. X Sees the Past   26

She Would Be a Teacher   28

And Peace Was My Companion   30

The House of Perfect Memories   32

Basements 34

The Stranger   37

An Angel in the Kitchen   39

The Sighting   41

Mother Has High Hopes   43

The Middle-age Overture   46

The Icky Mama Face   48

Mrs. X Gets an Idea   50

Mrs. X Cooks a Roast   52

Where the Lost Things Go   54

A Nose by Any Other Name Could Be a Popcorn Holder   56

A Dream and a Wish   58

Trying It On for Size   61

My Problem Now 63

The Gift   65

Mrs. X Surprises the Congregation   67

Motherjokes   69

Mrs. X Accepts a Challenge   71

Coming Home   74

Just One Day   77

A Visit from the Iceman   79

Cleopatra in the Dark   81

The Passing   83

The First Walker Theorem of Motherly Confusion 85

Mrs. X Barks Back   87

Cat Scratch Fever?   89

I Run Over It (Once)   91

I Run Over It (Twice)   93
The Perfectionist Makes a Mistake   95
Beverly Hits a High Note   97
Mrs. X Hears a Voice   99
Lavatoriphobia   101
Rockin' Without The Perfectionist   103
My Goose Gets Cooked   105
The Hock-A-Loogie Chorus   108
Baked to Perfection   110
Mrs. X Gets the Creeps   112
The Find   114
The Kiss   116
Mrs. Lookadoo   118
I Am Launched   120
Miscarriage   122
The Imaginary Hug   124
Freedom   126
An Ice Jacket Full of the Sun   128
The Standard for Courage 133
To The Perfectionist   135
Mrs. X's Soul Mate Takes Flight   137
About the Author 140

To Margaret Amidon Crawford,
my mother

The Pearl

Who made God?

It is early on a black November night, and only one dim lamp is in use. Burning in a corner, it casts a yellow glow over white walls and dusty furniture and a giant pile of our wrinkled but patient laundry.

I slip one hand around my iron's handle, and I grasp it firmly, touching its hot metal face with one spit-moistened finger.

Sssss.

The iron announces its readiness with a hiss, and I lay it down and push it back and forth across a blouse with a distinct but silent rhythm.

It is the rhythm of life. Things are smooth here. They look a little rough there. This section of life needs mending.

Behind me, stretched out on my bed, sits a long, slender boy who is as pliable as an old folding chair. His legs are collapsed upon themselves up under his seat, his feet are at angles, and his face is cast down, his large dark eyes watching his fingers at work.

They pull at tiny drawers, and they open and close boxes, searching for a mother's treasure.

He cannot know, because he is too young, that my treasure does not lie within them. I don't bother to tell him, though. Treasure is not something that can be explained.

There are many things in my aging jewelry box that capture his imagination, and he has begged for the privilege of looking there. On this night I have granted him permission.

He pulls out, first, a great, long shell necklace that harks back several generations, and he wonders aloud why anyone would want a necklace that goes on forever. The necklace continues where his great-great-great aunt left off, and it is longer than his upper body.

He dangles it before himself for effect, perhaps imagining the many dances it has attended, and then he returns it to its drawer, placing it in a pile.

I hear the tiny drawer close and others open. Costume pins appear and disappear without much fanfare. A class ring is produced and tried on a finger. A bracelet slides onto a skinny wrist, and some old coins that tempt him greatly come out of an aging Christmas holder.

The old coins have as much value as sentiment, but that is another unexplainable thing.

"Why don't you ever wear any of this stuff?" this curious boy asks. "If you're not going to wear it, why don't you give it away?"

He doesn't really want me to give it away. He wants me to give it to him. And I know this.

He is surprised when he pulls open a center drawer and finds two black and white ultrasound photos that represent him in the womb. They are under a souvenir bracelet from the Alamo and a pin that his grandma once wore.

Given ten years of age, the ultrasound pictures are slightly faded, and they are greatly wrinkled.

I set down my iron, and I take them from him. I smooth them with my fingertips and turn them around in my hands—they are the nearest thing to treasure in the box—and I point to them and say, "This is you before you were born."

This boy squints and he says, "Yuck."

His own image is not nearly as fascinating to him as my old charm bracelet, which contains everything, he says, that he has ever wanted: A spinning wheel. A hand pump. An hour glass. A dog. A clarinet. A spaceship. A watch. A crown.

He sulks for a minute before placing the bracelet back in its drawer (he dares to wonder who will get it when I am dead), and he searches out my pearl necklace.

Shimmering across his slim splayed fingers, the stringed pearls slide like water, and he watches them as the single lamp casts its yellow onto them, making them glow warm.

"Why would Jesus want a jewel to come out of an oyster?" this boy asks, directly.

I consider his face, which is now across from mine. I consider its innocence and its trust.

This is an important question, I know.

The pearl is a symbol, I tell him. It is like faith, or love, or even a mother's treasure.

It is the beautiful thing that grows where beauty is least expected.

Everyboy

Where do we get our energy from?

He is Everyboy: Eyes that monopolize his face, bowl haircut, mischievous smile, trusting heart.

He slips from his bed and creeps cautiously into the hallway as little boys so often do. His pajamas drag the floor just a little. His belly is exposed. His eyes are heavy with a need for sleep.

He passes his father and older sisters, silently, in search of me. He believes that I can do all things.

His room is a simple white and, though it has one window, it becomes very dark at night. He sleeps in a hand-me-down bed that is much too big for him.

Sometimes, I think his ears are too big for him too.

While he is not afraid of the dark, per se, he is made anxious by the noises that accompany it. He hears them all: Popcorn making its way, three rooms distant, around a bag in the microwave at 10 p.m. (*Can I have some?* he calls down the hall); his father sneaking out the front door for a late-night cigarette (*Are you guys going somewhere?*); his sister turning the knob that makes her bedside lamp shine (*Mom, she's out of be-hed!*).

It is a summer night, warm and humid, and the windows and doors are thrown open to let in the descending cool air.

We have no streetlights to ward off the creatures that thrive on darkness, and they make their way from a nearby woods as soon as the sun has set.

Sometimes, they work themselves across our sidewalk or even up the sides of our house, where we occasionally catch them peering in those very same windows. Most, however, stay in the grass where they make singing a nightly ritual.

He has been in the bed for only a few minutes when he emerges. He finds me on the couch, behind a book, a solitary light keeping me company.

The nighttime chorus has begun, but I do not notice it.

Perhaps I am not aware because I am too engrossed in my book. Perhaps I have learned to take nature's music for granted. Perhaps my ears are failing.

He comes up beside me and looks at me, trying to discern whether or not he will get a reprimand.

"What do you want?" I ask him, and I am only slightly impatient. I find it difficult to get angry when he casts those big, trusting eyes my way.

He says something that I don't quite understand at first. He still has, occasionally, the garbled speech of a toddler.

He makes his request again and motions outside to make his point.

"Would you turn off the crickets?" he asks. "They're keeping me awake."

I am stunned by his profound confidence in my abilities.

"Only God can silence the crickets," I tell him.

He scurries off to bed, satisfied, and goes quickly into a peaceful sleep. I turn back to my book, glad at the end of a long day that I have a greater power to defer to.

Busted Things

Have you ever had that distraction where your eyes are looking at something but you're not thinking anything?

Recently, The Perfectionist huffed the following to me: "You're getting to be more and more like your mother."

He made the remark during dinner and, honestly, I can't remember what it was that drove him to it.

Anyway, his observation set a pensive tone for the days that followed. I spent them, six in all, watching myself carefully and asking all too frequently while over the vacuum cleaner, the washing machine, or the garbage pail, "Have I been complimented or insulted?"

Alas, the answer came to me one evening as I sat watching my three-year-old son color. He had a large piece of white notebook paper before him and, in his hand, a broken piece of chalk, the color of which he could not identify.

He had used the chalk to draw a huge, bulging circle on the paper, and he had placed two uneven eyeballs up near its scalp.

He looked up at me (I wasn't paying much attention) and without speaking went back to his work, coloring in an oblong nose directly between the eyes.

After a spell he finally asked me, "What color is this?" And he held the chalk up for me to see at close range.

Evening was settling over the house and, in the ensuing darkness, I had difficulty making it out exactly.

The chalk was reddish, but it wasn't really red. I knew that if I said "red" he would debate the issue with me. He knows his reds, and he has a bit of The Perfectionist's personality.

I decided my best option was to give him an obscure answer. Reaching back into my own childhood, I pictured an array of sixty-some brand new crayons, fresh from their box with perfect points and their names written on the wrappers, and I said, admittedly stretching things a bit, "That's burnt sienna."

Just as I had hoped, he accepted my reply without qualms—without even asking me what burnt sienna means—and he returned to the picture, drawing pupils in the eyes and then furiously coloring in that part called "the whites."

After he had scribbled in all but a tiny speck in the right eye, he looked up at me, and motioning to his own eye with the chalk, said with a squint, "What do you call those busted things?"

I looked at him, and he motioned again.

"Busted things?" I asked. I couldn't imagine what he was talking about. "You mean the eyelashes?"

He became frustrated and pointed at his eye a third time. "You know, the busted things. The busted things. You've got 'em," he said, finally jabbing the chalk at me. "They're red."

How can I explain the revelation that took place? I mean, I had a Buddha-like experience right there in my own living room.

Immediately, and without question, I realized he was drawing a portrait of me, and that he was referring to the broken veins that punctuate my eyes.

"That kid doesn't miss a thing," I mumbled to myself, getting up to go check on my cooking dinner.

Mother's image walked with me to the kitchen.

"We never see ourselves as others see us," she's always said.

A Mother's Faith

Do you have any idea when night starts?

There came one Christmas Eve a gentle rapping at our front door, long after the setting of the sun.

The rap came, and came again, as we ate dinner. And we all paused, our forks stalled in mid-air, to listen while my mother said, "Now, who could that be?"

"Carolyn," she said, "why don't you go see who's knocking?"

I went but I could see nothing, for the tiny window that graced our front door towered high over my head.

I used both hands to twist the door's knob back and forth until it finally relented, opening with a great sucking sound to reveal one very chilled visitor on our front porch.

I looked at him, turned, and left him standing there, framed by snow and the blackest of skies, breathing frosty breaths into the night air.

"It's Santa Claus," I reported solemnly to those waiting in the kitchen.

And Mother, stifling a mixture of anticipation and exasperation, said (as if I was a hopelessly lost cause): "Well, why don't you let him in?" I complied, facing what I recall as my first encounter with one of life's mysteries: Why was Santa Claus shivering on our front porch at dinnertime and where, exactly, were his reindeer?

It could be said that my mother's faith and zest for life—the same ideals she hoped to instill in her daughters—were put to the test that evening in 1955. She had, after all, publicly displayed her trust by responding to a most unusual letter.

We had moved into our house only a few months before. A new, three-bedroom ranch, it sat in the middle of a line of matching houses.

They were the creations of a balding Englishman who bragged that he had come to America to seek his fortune with just a suitcase and five dollars to his name.

Only the most simple of things distinguished these houses from one another. Some had carports and some had garages. Some had gray bricks, and some had red. Some had cats, and some had dogs.

One day during the week before Christmas, the unsigned, handwritten letter appeared in our mailbox. It read: "If you believe in Santa Claus, put a red ribbon on your door."

No explanation accompanied the note, nor did any promises. Mother, ever hopeful, hung a red ribbon anyway.

Santa Claus made the rounds of every house with a ribbon that night.

Mother still recalls that Christmas Eve as the most beautiful she has ever seen.

A black sky full of stars illuminated the whitest of snows, and so our neighborhood, she says.

I remember it all with the greatest affection.

After Santa's departure, I went into my bedroom and stood by the window. Looking up, I hoped to catch a glimpse of him soaring over the neighborhood rooftops, laughing from the front of his sleigh as his reindeer pulled it along.

Instead, I saw only the sky, alive with stars that burned like the flames of candles. They flickered around a great star that shined boldly and did not waver.

In searching for Santa, I had surely found the Star of Bethlehem. It shined through a slit in my bedroom curtains and onto me as I slipped into my bed.

How easily my faith embraced this series of events.

How easily my mother gave that faith to me.

Realities

Do you know what being afraid is?

She's seven now. But I still go into her room at night to check on her and to watch her sleep.

She's usually scooched down to the end of the bed, under mounds of covers, her arms wrapped loosely around Ethel, the Cabbage Patch doll.

I stand over her in the stillness and watch her slow, rhythmic breathing. Sometimes I run my hand over her blond hair or kiss her cheek.

Always, I say a prayer. A prayer for her continued health, which was hard won but gracefully given. A prayer of thanksgiving that she is with us. A prayer for guidance in a situation I don't understand.

She sleeps through it peacefully . . . trusting.

I'm not sure when the bed-check ritual began. It may have started when she was born, and I stared through the window of the intensive care nursery at her little figure in the incubator, wondering what the world would have to offer when the odds seemed stacked against her.

"If she learns to talk . . . ."

"If she learns to walk . . . ."

The nurse's words echoed over and over.

It may have started late those nights when I worked in a hospital emergency room. I'd come home in the dark and snuggle under the covers with her and hold her tight, thankful that she wasn't the child who'd drowned or that she wasn't the little burned baby.

I think now that God placed me on that job during her first years for a reason. In the face of daily suffering and death, her poor eyes and her garbled speech didn't seem so bad.

I learned two things: There are always people who suffer, often courageously, more. And it can happen to anyone.

Sometimes when I'm watching her sleep, I think about all the years it took to teach her to eat with a fork or to climb the stairs or to pedal her bike.

I think about when she finally spoke her first word— "Mama" — to her father, at age two. Or the first time she said, "I love you," and I knew that she knew.

Sometimes, I think and marvel about the fact that she's really reading or about her simple, yet profound, faith.

When I think about that, I invariably think about the future.

What shall I tell her when she asks me why people call her a "retard"?

What shall I say when I lay dying?

Who shall I say is watching her . . . and praying?

Mrs. X Has a Religious Experience

Why do Sundays go by so quick?

Mrs. X was seated, though it went against her usual habit, on the second wooden pew from the front of the church. There were children on both sides of her and children to her front. They wriggled with boredom, and they kicked their feet, and they scratched themselves to the point that Mrs. X subconsciously began to scratch in unison.

She cast her eyes around the sanctuary.

"Let the little children come to me, and do not hinder them, for the kingdom of heaven belongs to such as these," was what Jesus had said to his followers.

Mrs. X sighed and thought about those words and the patience of the truly sainted.

Throughout her life, Mrs. X had never really been sure what she should do with her eyes when she was in church. She knew from her mother's teachings to cross her legs, ladylike, at the ankles. And she knew to fold her hands. And, on crowded days when the pews were full, she knew to keep her elbows flush against her ribs.

But where, exactly, did her eyes properly and reverently belong?

Mrs. X did not have a single answer.

Sometimes Mrs. X fixed her eyes on her folded hands, and she pondered them while the pastor spoke. When she was a child herself, she remembered, she had clenched them into little fist-sized churches and passed the time winding her fingers into imaginary steeples, playing a hand game long familiar to children.

It had been years since Mrs. X had played, she realized, and, impulsively, she clenched her hands shut once again and poked her two index fingers at one another. She was surprised at how aged and wrinkled they had become.

Sometimes, especially when the choir sang from beneath it, Mrs. X gazed rapturously at the cross hanging in the front of the sanctuary. Mrs. X felt most heavenly when she was surrounded by beautiful music. And she was certain during those times of song that an ethereal glow must go back and forth between the cross and her own face. There were Sundays when Mrs. X closed her eyes and basked in the warmth of that glow.

Other times, Mrs. X had to admit, she stared blankly at her fellow parishioners and wondered to herself how many of them were silently shushing their rumbling stomachs.

It was times like that, Mrs. X suspected, that she should have her eyes closed in prayer.

Though she had had girlhood notions, Mrs. X was well into her late thirties before she decided conclusively that she should close her eyes whenever she or someone else prayed.

Mrs. X knew God could hear the prayers of his people when their eyes were open. (After all, didn't he receive the prayers of frightened men as they marched, gape-eyed, off to war?) Still, it seemed to her that the closing of eyes during prayer time somehow made the act of worship all the more respectful.

And so she closed her eyes only to, on this particular Sunday, slip and let her right one peek.

A peek, Mrs. X soon realized, was nothing if not a full-blown temptation. For before she knew it, as if she had no real will of her own, Mrs. X had opened both eyes wide, and she was watching the little girl who sat before her.

The little girl had wriggled her way off the pew, and she was squatted behind a woman who knelt at the altar. The woman had her head bowed into one hand, and she clasped the railing with her other.

She was a plump, aging woman whose figure had begun to sag and whose bottom was, quite frankly, her greatest feature.

Mrs. X wondered what the woman was praying about—what worry she might be presenting to God—when she noticed the little girl inching forward. The little girl glanced at the other adults who were gathered at the altar and observed that some had their hands resting compassionately on the shoulders of others.

Thus inspired, the little girl reached out, and she attempted to place her small hand on the woman's distant shoulder.

Her fingers stretched into the air and they paused on the end of the little girl's too-short arm and then they fluttered down, coming to rest at last on the woman's greatest feature.

Mrs. X noticed that the woman did not react. Instead, she kept her head bowed into her hand and, if anything, went a little deeper into her prayer.

Mrs. X guessed that the touch of the child's hand must feel as gentle and as encouraging as that of an angel.

And she wondered, briefly, if God closes his own eyes when a child such as this attempts a laying on of the hands.

An Old Mother's Tale

Do you know how many skin cells it takes to make a wrinkle?

I can view pictures of my mother as a young woman and see a lot of myself in them.

I am there in her full-lipped smile and her green eyes and the peculiar twists of her short, wild hair.

The Perfectionist likes to think that he could see my future by watching my mother, way back when. It followed, he thought, that I would have her coloring and much of her shape, eventually.

Call it an old mother's tale.

"Look at a woman's mother and you will know what she is going to look like when she's older," I've heard him say to our oldest daughter, implying—much to her horror—that she will look like me someday.

I have always considered my mother to be beautiful.

Her size has fluctuated a little over the years, and her hair has faded from red to brown to white, but it still shines and so does she.

"How old are you?" my six-year-old son asked me the other night as he tossed down a drink of water before going to bed.

"I'm forty-three," I said.

Facts and figures (the mathematical kind) are just beginning to mean something to him.

He was intrigued, and he pushed his line of questioning further. "When will you be one hundred?"

He set down his glass and inched toward me.

I was a little surprised by the question and, of course, considering his delicate age, didn't want to tell him that I might never be one hundred.

That kind of information would devastate him.

"In fifty-some years," was the response I decided on.

It was honest. It made the decades seem light years away. And it would give him time to grow up and come to terms with the fact that death is a part of life.

I dragged a wet washrag around the counter and said, "Now go get into your pajamas."

My son was standing close to me by this time, and there were more questions to come.

"What will you look like?" he asked.

I thought of my mother. Well-groomed. Pleasantly colorful in her hair and lips. Full of life and an object of his affection.

My son is a lot shorter than I am. I put down my rag and walked toward him and bent over, lovingly. I ran my hands across my face as I prepared my answer.

"Oh, I'll probably have wrinkles and white hair," I said, only to learn that honesty is not the best policy at bedtime.

My son began to cry—deep, heartfelt sobs of grief that he could not control.

"Then I'm going to run away," he said.

Right now, I seem to be the most adored, wonderful person in his life.

We have never given words to the natural changes that must come to our relationship, and yet my son seems to sense that come they must.

Next time, I think I'll tell him that "a gentleman never asks a lady her age."

Some sage who lived before me wisely figured that one out.

Bewitched

Have you ever had your teeth jitter?

It seems that I came into being about the same time as early suburban subdivisions. When I was four years old my parents, like many others, moved from an old white, clapboard house in a dying city to a never-been-lived-in ranch house in a village.

To my child's eye, it looked as if a giant had taken a pair of cookie cutters and cookie sheets and laid out what was our street: Matching ranches on one block and matching colonials on the other.

If Paul Bunyan could stamp out Michigan with one press of his hand, as we children reasoned when we played, a lesser giant could perform that lesser feat.

Believing was such a simple matter back then.

Almost from the inception of subdivisions, a Halloween ritual developed. Children, clothed as ghosts or hula girls or firefighters or mummies forced down dinners on mothers' orders, while darkness settled over the neighborhood.

"No trick-or-treating on empty stomachs," was the cry that echoed up and down both sides of the street.

It was also generally understood that fathers would take their young children on their rounds. Mothers were left to hand out candy, and they performed their tasks predictably.

Porch lights were turned on. Inside doors were left ajar. Greetings were issued, and treats passed from behind swinging screen doors. Dogs were corralled to bark aimlessly from garages or distant bedrooms.

Only one mother, once, dared to vary from that pattern.

It was pitch black by the time we reached her.

Street lamps glowing from the block corners cast an eerie shine on, but did not really illuminate, her house. It loomed over us, bigger than big, and seemed to breathe in rhythm with the silhouetted trees that swayed in the wind around it.

"Go ahead. Go ahead," Father said to us when we balked at moving forward.

He stood at the curb with his hands plunged into his pants' pockets, blocking out the cold. And my younger sister and I inched our way, tentatively, up the driveway to stand before the mother's door.

The house, new as the others, was rickety and fearsome in the dead of night. And the porch seemed to sag under our combined weight.

"You ring the bell," I said.

"No, you do it," my sister replied.

The temptation to turn and run was strong, and we contemplated it, but not fast enough. The woman inside must have sensed our presence. She opened her door, slowly. And we waited, quite unprepared.

In a flash, camera ready, she turned on a light and leaned over us—a green-faced, ugly, hunching witch with candy in a twisted hand. She offered it to us through the space that had been her door's screen, without saying a word.

Oh, dread.

Should we take it? What if we touched her? What if she pulled us in?

My sister and I grabbed at the candy without looking to see what kind it was, and we threw back a pair of "thank you's" even as our feet began to race for the street.

"Dad," we panted to him, "that lady is a witch!"

Even in the darkness, we could sense the pleasure that settled over our oftentimes stern and brooding father.

Perhaps it was that night we first realized the safety of his arms.

A Halloween Surprise

What is a "faint"?

I've had a hard time decorating my bathroom. I've painted it twice and papered it twice in fifteen years.

When I picked out the countertop, I chose a color that had potential.

When I wallpapered, I went for mood. (What was warm and cozy to me was "too dark to shave in" for The Perfectionist.)

As it turns out, after all my hard work, it is a tiny, tree-shaped, adaptable toothbrush standing in a child-made vase that captures everyone's attention.

Especially my son's.

The dentist gave me the brush several years ago. It is designed to reach those hard-to-get-at spots between my teeth. I use it once in a while, but not as frequently as I'm supposed to.

Now what, you might justifiably ask, does that have to do with the Halloween holiday?

Geez, I shudder to think about it!

Recently, on a school morning, I happened to pass the bathroom, where my son was busy drying his hands in a most unusual way.

Peeking in a crack between the door and its frame, I caught him making wicked faces in the mirror and flailing his arms around, creating wind. (A born actor, he is forever practicing his "powers.")

"Better hurry up, you're going to be late," I said to him, pressing my face into the crack.

He picked up a towel quickly, on the defensive, and looked toward the crack.

"Hey, mom," he said, his voice exaggerating the words dramatically, "guess what?"

Well, let me tell you I couldn't begin to guess what. But my antennae did go up.

"What?" I asked him, making my way into the bathroom.

"One time," he said, again summoning as much drama as he was capable of, "that toothbrush" (at this point, he extended a crooked finger toward everyone's favorite conversation piece) "flew into the toilet!"

He whirred his arms once more.

I was stunned, nay, horrified. How many brushings ago had that happened? I wondered. I didn't really want to know.

I practice composure like he practices acting.

"Really?" I said, touching my hairdo nonchalantly with a look in the mirror. "And how did that happen?"

Again he picked up the towel. Swirling it through the air like a tornado, he said, arching his eyebrows for effect, "The towel flew around like this (whip, whip) and it got caught and just flew in the toilet."

He grinned up at me and told me about how he had rescued the toothbrush "a long time ago."

What can I say except, "Trick? Or treat?"

Mrs. X Sees the Past

Don't you just hate it when you get a hair in your way?

Mrs. X arched her back slightly as her hairdresser wound a plastic drape about her neck. It was stuffed with a towel for comfort and, as always, it fit tight, creating a three-layered tuft of fat under Mrs. X's chin.

Faced with her face in the mirror, Mrs. X considered herself: A plump light bulb in a cheap shade.

The oomph, oomph, oomph of the beautician's chair being pumped up under her weight distracted her briefly.

Each oomph told her she needed to diet.

While Mrs. X was aware that no one in the beauty shop was staring at her, she nevertheless felt unsightly and self-conscious. There was something about the entire beautifying process that unnerved her.

She looked down, flapped her arms to align the cape, folded her hands beneath it, stretched her neck and returned her eyes to the mirror.

Almost immediately her gaze fell upon a distant, reflected, plastic-enshrouded face from the past. She recognized the long, beaked nose, the thick eyebrows, even the Adam's apple straining to rise above the cape.

Reality dawned, and she was shocked.

There was her old high school biology teacher!

Mrs. X had always liked that teacher, even had a brief crush on him during her junior year. He was funny. Handsome. Attentive.

How long had it been since she had last thought of him?

Surprisingly, his face was still youthful. He had to be well over fifty years old, she thought. Yet there were few wrinkles and his eyes shown with merriment—as they had in the classroom—when he talked with the woman who was attending him.

Mrs. X watched, indeed she could not avert her eyes, as his beautician used a crochet hook to pull wet clumps of hair through the holes that dotted the rubber cap on his head. She massaged. She groped. Soon she was applying red coloring.

Within the hour, the biology teacher had a full head of unruly red curls!

Mrs. X was incredulous. For the first time in her life, she realized that the beautifying process had gone quickly.

No magazine article, no scandalous rumors circulating the shop had ever entertained her as completely and as satisfyingly as had the transformation of Mr. Rose.

Shampooed, trimmed and dried, Mrs. X eased herself happily out of her chair. She paid the clerk, hesitated, grinned to herself and decided, "What the heck!"

Mrs. X walked over to the teacher, who was still seated, and she loomed over him. (It was sinfully fun.) He looked up at her, and she stooped.

"Aren't you Mr. Rose from my old high school?" she asked.

Mr. Rose blushed as she knew he would.

She spoke with him briefly, reminding him of their days together, and she allowed herself to believe that he remembered.

That night, Mrs. X danced a tango with a red-haired stranger in her dreams.

She Would Be a Teacher

What do our souls look like?

My friend Jessica is ten years old. She has long, layered, curly brown hair, cheeks full of freckles and big blue eyes that light up her face when she giggles.

She knows already that she wants to be a teacher when she grows up.

Jessica will make an excellent teacher. She is bright, enthusiastic, patient and extremely good with people. Take this case in point:

Once we were strangers. But Jessica broke that barrier easily, as children do, when she offered to let me sleep in her bed when I had nowhere else to stay.

She, after all, would not be home to use it that week.

I slept peacefully in Jessica's room. Little-girl lavender, it takes up the lower, right rear corner of her house, and it gets a cross breeze that's perfect for sleeping on hot nights.

It's the envy of her brothers and sister.

Jessica has given her room ambiance by filling it with her treasures: scads of stuffed animals, a bell collection, an award for getting her tonsils out and a basket full of shells and rocks.

She spent an hour with me one morning, telling me she got this shell here and that shell there, and the reasons why they are all very precious.

For the most part, everything is neat and tidy in Jessica's bedroom. There's a box of toys that needs to be sorted, and her mother complains about the condition of the closet.

But then, do you know a mother who doesn't complain about such things?

Jessica's mother, Mary Ann, is remarkable in the same loyal, work hard, anonymous way that many women are. She's a single parent, and she's raising four children, two dogs and three cats, essentially alone, while working a full-time job.

Somehow she manages to squeeze scouts and Jessica's horseback riding lessons into her schedule.

One night after we'd visited Jessica and my daughter at the hospital where they shared a room, I told Mary Ann that I thought Jessica was an amazing child.

I told her how she was the first mentally normal child to play with my mentally retarded daughter in years. And that I was appreciative.

"That's because Jessica realizes she could have been retarded," Mary Ann said.

Jessica was born with spina bifida, a deformity of the spine that could have interfered with her mental as well as physical development.

Jessica has a shunt in her head that drains off a build-up of spinal fluid, thankfully leaving her with an above-normal intelligence.

She has been through seven grueling operations to repair her spine and improve the walking she does with crutches. The last one took ten hours. She has at least one more to go.

Jessica faces these challenges with a courage and charm that I find remarkable.

It gives me shudders when I think of the advice a doctor gave Mary Ann soon after Jessica's birth.

He said, "If this was my child, I would starve her to death."

And Peace Was My Companion

How high is heaven?

The little, four-year-old girl next door is a child after my own heart. She would just as soon be up a tree as not.

She is squat (she leads with her belly) and solid and, being so young, she cannot get into a tree without the assistance of an adult.

The tree she most often chooses for climbing is a young maple that shades a small portion of her front yard. I suppose there is a challenge to climbing that tree, and safety to be had on home turf. Fear is not really a big factor.

The tree was planted by men who constructed her house, and every other house on our street.

They made a spectacle of their tree-planting one blustery winter day long before the little girl was born. I watched them in amazement. Chipping at holes in the frozen earth. Planting seedlings for each family in a haze of snow. Kicking ice and hard soil into place around the trees' balled roots.

Yet, somehow the trees, like the neighborhood, flourished.

Hefting this little girl into her tree's arms is like balancing a fifty-pound bag of potatoes on a fence post. First there is the lifting. Then there is the shifting.

Once she has anchored herself into the crotch of the tree, where three good branches meet some seven feet off the ground, she is full of wonderment.

She is taller than an adult. She can touch a passing plane. She is ever more aware that there is a heaven. It spreads itself above her and it is blue.

I envy her, for I was forced to give up tree-climbing when I was fourteen years old.

I had a favorite tree that I used to climb that towered way over the house where I lived. To get into it, I had to climb halfway up another tree and make a daring switch from the branches of the first to the second.

I always climbed as far up the tree as I could. To the point where the tree's branches turned into delicate limbs that would not support my weight.

From that vantage point, well above the roof of my home, I was master of all that I surveyed. And peace was my companion.

One day—I remember it vividly—my mother walked from the kitchen to the dining room (I could see her, a little ant, passing from one window to another). She opened the sliding glass door and stepped out into the sunshine and shook her finger up at me and shouted, "You come down from that tree! You're getting too big to climb trees."

I was dumbfounded. I came down from the tree and asked for an explanation.

Somehow, it all had to do with the fact that ladies do not climb trees.

Looking back on her demand, I realize how unnecessary it was. The same Nature that called me to that tree eventually called me to other interests.

The way I see it, my little neighbor has a good twelve to fifteen years of tree-climbing ahead of her. I'll give her a boost as long as she needs one.

And as long as my back holds out.

Nature will probably have something to say about that, too.

The House of Perfect Memories

Do you know why I wish we lived on a cloud?

The tree still stands, despite what must have been great odds. It looks out over the dusty road, its arms reaching, as if it expects that someday soon children will return to it.

It has kept this lonely vigil now for years.

Around it, what is left of a family farm slowly goes to ruin. Weeds and wildflowers grow haphazardly. The frame of a tottering swing-set, with no swings, leans to the right and rusts.

The old shingled chicken coop leans too.

Sometimes I drive out to visit the place. I always draw up alongside the road's shoulder and sit. I never venture onto the property. I can see all that I need to from there, even with my eyes closed.

I am beside my mother in our 1955 Pontiac. She angles the car onto the driveway, it bounces in a few ruts, then dips into a hollow and rises close to the farmhouse just behind the tree.

Sandy is on the back steps, holding a kitten, and I am at her side as fast as my feet can carry me.

A cacophony of animals and people and machinery surrounds us.

This, I have no doubt, is heaven.

Sandy and I hurry into the house. We have a weekend ahead of us—not long enough—and we are anxious to begin.

We pass through a small back room that houses a few chickens, through the kitchen and the living room and bolt up a flight of steep stairs to her bedroom.

Two single beds are shoved against the right-hand wall. Across from them, bookcases hold an enticing array of Nancy Drew books. Beside the far bed, under a window, sits the dollhouse that Sandy shares with her sister. It is resplendent with a variety of tiny furnishings and working utensils.

There will be time to read and play dolls after dark, we decide. After all, who will be able to sleep with her father's thunderous snoring rising through the vent in the floor?

We throw my suitcase onto her bed and hurry to take advantage of the remaining daylight. We run through fields, climb the fallen-down log, inspect the barn, dodge first an angry bull and then her brothers.

I, in my city-bred naivetè, have no way of knowing that Sandy has been up since 4:30 a.m., when she made her rounds feeding animals. Or that she wore her school clothes to bed the night before so she wouldn't have to get dressed in the chill of that hour.

Sitting in my car as an adult, I marvel at how much I envied her life.

Animals, a crowd of siblings and freedom were all I saw. How did I miss the endless labor that went into maintaining a farm? How could I not see the discord that separated her parents?

After their divorce, the farm was sold. A short time later, reportedly in just fifteen minutes, a raging fire claimed the house and all that was left behind waiting to be moved, including the doll-house.

The tree, a giant pine, somehow survived, despite its close proximity to the house. It is scorched up its backside, obscenely.

Time was, you could gather children beneath it to plan strategies, pitch knives and tell secrets. It was so wide and thick, you could relax in its shade on a hot summer day or imagine the best of Christmases about it in winter.

It was also so tall that you could look out into its midst from Sandy's bedroom window, even as you worked out lives in the tiny dollhouse.

The view from my car window pales by comparison. The only advantage I have is that I can always close my eyes.

Basements

What does the "heebie-jeebies" mean?

There is an oppression about this hot summer day. Musty city air hangs heavily over us, so thick that my sister and I believe that we can control it with a touch. We reach our fingers out to push it away and the air pretends, briefly, to take flight at our commands.

"Be gone!" we say. And it moves.

Then we create little funnels that are in actuality no more ominous than our whirring arms. These breezes of our making provide no real relief and, ultimately, it is the air that has the final say. It settles back around us, spread out like water in a barrel, contained only by the shimmering city walls and streets.

Old city houses lean against the air and look wilted.

Our aunt's house is a gray monolith against the gray sky that oversees this scene. Inside of it, she wipes her hands on her apron, brushes a wet curl from her forehead, and wipes her hands again. We watch this act through our aunt's kitchen window.

She places her dish towel on a wall rack and steps toward the back door. She pushes it open and promenades herself onto the back stoop. She is wearing a dark-colored, white-flowered dress that calls to mind her vastly-flowered yard on a moonlit night. Her dog, Lady, comes out the door with her.

Speaking to us about things that I cannot remember, our aunt puts a hand over her eyes to protect them, and she tilts her face upward toward the sky. She surveys great storm clouds that are rolling pell-mell toward us, and she waits quietly for the first drops of rain. They are the drops of rain that we hope will cool this sweltering day.

When they come, at long last, they come with a clap of thunder that makes Lady cower. They drip at first like a leaky faucet. And then they rain faster. And the gentle, beautiful Lady is afraid.

"Lady doesn't like storms," our aunt tells us. She steps down off the stoop with an arthritic lurch and takes the dog by her collar, moving her toward a door in the ground that leads to our aunt's basement.

She lifts it up to reveal a little room that is but one part of the basement, urges Lady down its few steps, and calls us in behind them. Into Lady's sanctuary. Into the darkness. She closes the door and we walk along a cold, cement floor into the greater rooms of the basement, past the shadows of gardening tools that line up against the walls under tiny, dirty windows. Past old wicker baskets. Past spiderwebs that touch our faces. Past home-canned peaches and pears that float in their own juices in clear jars. The fruit has been floating for years, as evidenced by the collection of dust on the jar lids.

The jars climb up layers of shelves, and we wonder how the old people who live in this house could ever possibly eat all that fruit. We wonder if they could live long enough. Then we reach our fingers out to swipe across the dust.

We are standing in a line: A border collie, an old woman, two little sisters.

Another roll of thunder bangs its way over our aunt's house and Lady pushes herself against the basement floor with a whimper. Our aunt pets her long, black fur by way of comfort, and Lady puts her muzzle into my aunt's palms.

All around us are the remnants of concurrent lifetimes. Cane poles. Hoes. A wheelbarrow. Broken chairs. A hose. A shovel. Empty suitcases.

Our aunt pulls a string dangling from a light bulb and it lurches on, swinging from a chain down from the ceiling. It casts a yellow glow over the remnants, over us, over the dog, and for a few brief moments, we are not one, but four Ladies on a trek, having an adventure in a secret cavernous land.

I stand at the far end of my basement. It is cooler than the rest of the house. I pull the light bulb string and bring darkness down around myself. The familiar transform into black, hulking beasts.

I put my hands out about me and fumble my way toward the stairway that I know is there. I feel my ankle brush against the coarse edges of an open cardboard box. I hurry a little as my imagination gets the better of me.

The whole house has my touch, but even that cannot keep me safe. As I hurry toward the staircase, I hear a footstep fall across the kitchen floor above me and a board creaks. I hurry faster, away from whatever it is that's chasing me.

My basement gives me the creeps as most basements do.

They are not like my aunt's basement—now languishing beneath the footfalls of strangers who know nothing of the safety, of the kindness, of the bonding, of the wishes, and of the memories that took place there.

The Stranger

What is a chill?

It is the mid-1950s. A small girl, perhaps five or six years of age, walks a dog on a city sidewalk that fronts, in addition to other buildings, three towering two-story houses.

The girl has honey-blond hair that is pulled into two thick braids that lie awkwardly atop her shirt collar. A breeze brushes her and blows stray strands into her face. She pays no attention.

She concentrates, instead, on her hands, which are wrapped tightly around a dog's leash. They do not really restrain the animal. It has no desire to run away.

The dog is a black border collie with a touch of white and brown on its chest. It walks slowly, close to the child and occasionally tilts its head up to look in her face.

The girl is smiling and murmuring to the dog. They share an obvious affection for one another. They are alone, together. And they are taking their first unsupervised stroll with the three houses acting as their boundaries.

The houses, silver, dark gray, and yellow, respectively, are beginning to sag with age and use.

The silver house has been used the most. People move into and out of it endlessly. They always seem to be fighting. Doors slam and voices can be heard at all hours, trying to out-shout other voices.

The house gives anxiety to the street and keeps its neighbors from becoming too comfortable.

A quiet couple lives in the yellow house. They have for a long time. They tend a garden and park their car in an alley that runs alongside their city lot.

They treat the lady who lives in the middle house with kindness. It is a kindness that goes a long, long way.

The little girl belongs, sort of, to that lady. She is the sister of the little girl's mother. She has never married or had children of her own, so she happily treats the little girl as if she were hers.

And she owns the dog.

While the child and the dog are walking, a large green car moves up parallel to them. It does not pull over to the curb but remains in the middle of the road.

There is only one man in the car. He is youngish, and he has dark hair that blurs with the car's shadowy interior. The man pushes open the driver's door just a fraction, with the car's motor still running, and he calls out to the little girl.

He is offering her a piece of candy in exchange for a closer look at the collie.

The little girl stops, tempted, and starts toward the street. She begins to step out before remembering her mother's admonishment: never go to strangers.

Suddenly she shouts a "No!" and runs, tugging at the dog, for the refuge of the middle house. She bounds up the porch stairs, throws open the front door and falls into the safety of the living room.

All the while she can hear tires crunching in the gravel of the alley next door, then screeching away.

I would flee to the dark gray house again if I could.

An Angel in the Kitchen

Why do people cry when they're happy?

Shivering in the cool fall air, I step away from my grandmother's front stoop and fairly glide across the threshold that leads into her evergreen-colored living room. (It is her aging daughter's really, for my grandmother never owned a house in her lifetime.) A welcoming fire licks at the fireplace walls across from where I glide, but even its familiar and thick scents cannot compete with those filtering in from the kitchen.

The aroma of cooking bean soup beckons me with invisible airborne fingers, like those of a well-perfumed ghost. They are salty, heavy, heavenly.

I hurry away from my mother, who is hanging jackets, and I run through the dark and quiet rooms to find my grandmother working, as is her lot in life. Her back is to me and her old dog, Lady, panting at her side, spies me first.

Lady acknowledges me with a look but does not venture away from my grandmother. Perhaps the dog, too, is tempted by the beans.

Short and plump and absolutely erect, my grandmother stands before her stove, concentrating on the contents of a large black kettle. She is under five feet tall, and the gas burners of the stove rise beneath her breasts as if they intend to offer up some kind of support—but my grandmother seems unaware of this.

Together, Lady and she are silhouetted by a back door window that overlooks my aunt's expansive flower garden. The yellow daisies of my grandmother's threadbare housedress dance and sway with her cooking motions. They seem ever more beautiful and eternal to me than those that were so well-tended outback during the summer.

Absentmindedly, my grandmother runs a hand across the skirt of her dress, pushing it against her thigh, then she angles an elbow up awkwardly into the air in order to reach over the kettle's lip and stir the beans. Neither the effort of the reach, nor the day spent on her feet deter her. Nor does the increasing heat of the kitchen or the prospect of feeding several hungry guests.

They have gathered, one at a time, in the living room to await this time-honored family staple, which will include two sides of chopped onions and buttered homemade rolls. The bean soup meal is as familiar to them as the old family photos that hang on the walls. And just as cherished.

Pushing a large wooden spoon around and around with one hand, my grandmother raises the other hand to brush a sweat-drenched, white curl from her forehead.

She then nudges her glasses back up to the bridge of her nose, from where they've slipped, and I watch as she fishes a single bean onto a spoon.

She looks at it, still unaware that I am present, then gingerly places it between her front teeth, bites down, and tests it for doneness.

The bean, done, burns her lips slightly, and she quickly fans the pain away with her aged fingers.

"Ooh!" she says, and the dog perks her ears.

The intimacy of this moment fills me with emotion that I cannot contain. I hurry to throw my arms around her thick waist, my small hands crinkling the daisies that adorn her.

Quietly, she releases her spoon into the soup and turns to embrace me, stroking my hair.

As she does so, steam from the kettle rises and surrounds her face as I know a halo would.

The Sighting

Wouldn't it be cool if we were ghosts?

You expect apparitions, if you believe in such things, to appear out of nowhere sometimes. But you do not expect the same of old ladies.

Nevertheless, two of them, similar in shape and color, showed themselves on our front porch one Sunday afternoon very long ago.

It has been more than thirty years since the sighting, and we still have no idea where they came from, anymore than we know where they were going.

Father turned our Pontiac easily, quietly, onto the driveway as he always did to avoid jarring it on the slight uphill approach to our house. And we got out of the car, as we always did, four adult-sized family members from four doors, and we walked toward the house lost in our individual thoughts.

We did not expect to be brought out of those thoughts by the backsides of two elderly women, stooped and unknown to us, who stood peering—with their hands shading their eyes—into the picture window that fronted our living room.

It being a Sunday, they were clean and well-dressed, as if they had just come from church. Each had on a white blouse and a skirt, subdued in color to complement the graying in their hair, and each carried a purse slung over a forearm.

They didn't speak to one another or move about. They only looked for what seemed like the longest time into the place that we called home.

Stunned by this invasion of our privacy, we stood and watched as they gleaned what they could of our lives.

What could they possibly have been looking for? A glimpse at how the other half lives? A likeness of the homes they once kept?

Ours was an average house. Brick and wood. Relatively new. Safe from leaks. A birch tree in back. A pine tree in front. Honeysuckle flowers to taste on summer evenings.

Had we been in there going about our business, the ladies would have seen only ordinary people doing ordinary things: Petting the cat, reading the paper, talking.

Maybe they were wistful.

After a while, the women must have sensed that our eyes were upon them. They turned together, toward us, and cast their eyes to the ground in a combination of guilt and shame.

Caught!

Being elderly, they had no choice but to walk the length of the sidewalk that joined our house to the driveway and then past us to the road to make their escape. There would be no vaulting over the hedges. No racing across the lawn.

They gripped their pocketbooks tightly in their hands and dared in their embarrassment to give us a nod of acknowledgment as they left. There were no comments.

We watched while they walked by the car (they avoided it carefully) and while they moved onto the street, slow but determined.

Gradually their forms blended with the colors and shapes in the distance.

Two apparitions out for a stroll.

Mother Has High Hopes

Why is it rainbows only have five colors?

My father saw red one summer early in my youth, when city shops flourished instead of malls, and "up north" Michigan was a fantasyland, and the problems in our lives could be wadded into a single, strong palm and shoved into one of his deep, warm pockets.

It was a summer when I believed that my mother could do no wrong. Back when it was becoming clear to me that her natural gifts were for leadership and courage.

It was back when she was the woman I longed to someday be.

The summer came with scorching, sun-filled days that burnt our skin and temperate nights that brought comfort with them. We went into those nights with Frank Sinatra songs playing in the background, and rattle-trap cars honking on the distant highway, and our parents' soft evening discussions lulling us to sleep.

In those days, Frank Sinatra sang about "High Hopes."

Back then I had really good hair. It fell to my waist like a honey-colored waterfall and after a vigorous washing—with fingers that she had strengthened doing daily typing—my mother would rinse it with a combination of vinegar and water to make it shine. Then, for drying purposes, she would send me out to our swings to set it free.

I dried my hair like I haven't dried it since. I launched my swing with a great push of my feet against the yard, and I aimed my head for the heavens.

My hair liked it up there. It always trailed me at a distance when I swung back down to earth.

On some of those aforementioned nights, my hair, even though clean, would cake itself against my back and make my neck sweat so that I wished my mother would cut it off.

During the day, my mother twisted it into merciless braids that gave a permanent set of happiness to my face.

Braids like those, these days, would pull away my deepening crow's feet.

I have a mental image of myself standing beside my mother in a men's clothing department in a busy downtown store. It is one of those scorching days, and I am looking up at her and my eyes are "set" —even as they marvel at what she's doing.

She holds up before her—like you would a big bed sheet when you're hanging it on a clothes line—a pair of fire-engine-red men's pants. She is sizing them up with great interest, and a smile of temptation is overriding her face.

In my mental image she does not speak. Instead, she surveys the pants and flexes their waistband and tests their legs' durability with a forceful shake, and then she goes, "Hmm."

The pants, in my mental image, fairly glow.

Temptation, I understand now from the vantage point of age, plays its role in the qualities of leadership and courage. Surely a woman must visualize the possibilities and want to seize them before she can take action.

And so my mother, standing there and visualizing in an age and time when bright colors were not worn by men, conjured a mental image of her own. She envisioned my father—a quiet, decent man who lived his life in shades of browns and blues—adorned in red.

And she made her purchase.

That night (my mother's face was alight with expectation), my father shunned the red pants. There was no way. And that was that.

If temptation is the forerunner of leadership and courage, determination is their companion.

Mother bided her time until that summer's vacation up north— with my father, it would seem, still trusting her. For he requested, perhaps without thinking, that she pack his suitcase on his behalf.

That she pack all the clothes he would need to enjoy himself for two weeks.

What my father needed, my mother decided, were his red pants. And so she packed them—and them alone—folding them into a tight, little bundle.

Later, and hundreds of miles from home, Father had no choice but to wear the red pants.

Probably, my parents hoped that I would remember something of Michigan's history from that vacation. Something of its bears and foxes and its Native Americans and its pioneers and forts and scenery.

Instead, what I see when I think of it, is my father standing on a beach at Lake Superior, casting his fishing line against a scene of deep blue water and towering green pines, glowing with the red of those pants.

Off in the distance I envision Mother, too. She is smiling and humming along with Frank.

The Middle-age Overture

Is it true if you run fast enough, smoke can come behind you?

"Ta Da Dum. Ta Da Dum. Ta Da Dum, Dum, Dum"
—*The William Tell Overture.*

During my childhood, when the melodic strains of the *William Tell Overture*—familiar to baby boomers as the Lone Ranger theme song from television's 1950s—echoed throughout our home early on Sunday mornings, it was not a "Hi Yo, Silver!" that we heard following the last "ta, da, dum, dum, dum."

It was an exasperated, frenetic and unfeminine, "Francis Eugene!"

My father, by all accounts a quiet and a gentle man, loved being a piano subversive.

He would do as so many men do on Sunday mornings when they don't really want to climb out from under their warm blankets, or go start their cold cars, or get on their knees and pray.

He would put on his shirt and his pants, his socks and his shoes and his tie and his suit jacket and brush his teeth. Then, with malice aforethought, he would go down the few steps into our family room while my mother went about the sometimes lengthy task of getting the rest of us ready for church services.

He would seat himself at our awkward old upright piano and allow his hands to dance across its keys, nimbly tapping out tunes from memory—all up and down the keyboard—that he had used to lure my mother during their war-years' courtship.

Sometimes he would play songs of his own creation—songs that came so effortlessly from his fingertips that I realize, now, they were literally a part of him. They had an ease and a flair about them that spoke of a younger man who I could never really know.

I can remember sitting at his side on the piano bench (it was gigantic then) and watching his fingers and thumbs as they worked, coaxing first the love songs and then the ta, da, dum, dum, dums.

My mother was a victim of her own sense of rhythm. Ask those who know her and they will tell you that no music ever passed her way that she did not seize its tempo, snap her fingers and sway her body in appreciation.

My father knew this as surely as he knew that my mother too often got her own way.

The William Tell Overture, clearly, was not written to be a part of Sunday morning worship. There is nothing pensive or soothing or reverent about it. Nothing in it that encourages a spiritual light to shine—or that soothes the soul.

With its staccato notes and its rapid-fire pace, it was conceived, I'm sure, to motivate armies. At our house it motivated my mother as well.

I think that perhaps my father stumbled upon the song's power quite by accident. And once realized, it quickly became his ally.

He would begin slowly and softly at about 7:30 a.m., his fingertips lightly dancing across the keys. (I can picture him still: a slim man in a dress shirt, his black hair slicked away from his face, his brown eyes intent on what his hands were doing.)

Then he would accelerate—his hands moving swiftly and with more assurance, the notes coming louder and at a fiercer rate. "Ta, da, dum. Ta, da, dum. Ta, da, dum, dum, dum. Ta, da, dum. Ta, da, dum. Ta, da, dum, dum, dum."

I watched—and felt my blood stir with excitement—while his face filled with glee and a little smirk came to his lips.

Up the stairs, my mother dashed by, a high-heeled shoe clutched in one hand.

To the west she went to double-check the kitchen faucet. To the east she went, in search of a hat. To the west she went again, this time a little faster. To the east, she was beginning to run.

Knowing that my mother couldn't help but subconsciously keep pace with his playing, my father forced the notes from the piano with a demonic pleasure, and he threw his head backward, and he pounded harder, and he let his eyes shift toward mine. We laughed in our hearts at his little form of rebellion, and we looked toward the top of the stairs.

Inevitably my mother would stand above us, bent forward, scowling down and panting, out of breath.

"Francis Eugene!" she huffed and the words carried the weight of a scolding.

"Francis Eugene!" she huffed again and my father shrugged and he said, "What?"—though he knew perfectly well.

The Icky Mama Face

What is a sermon?

The little girl behind the mother's frustration was a blue-eyed, pouty-lipped, curly-haired blonde.

Legs and arms jutted out of her stroller like unrestrained spokes from a wheel. A hand here. A foot there. Another hand over there.

Touch a display case. Kick at a dress. Wiggle. Wiggle. Wiggle.

Like all toddlers, she had curiosity, speed and daring on her side.

And like all mothers who are divested of their patience, the child's mother was reaching the upper bounds of her frustration threshold.

"Don't touch that, or . . . ." the mother said to the little girl as she reached out to fondle a rack of women's clothing, "I'll show you the icky mama face."

That did it.

No smack on the hands, no pinch, no heavy-duty scolding was needed. Obediently, the child put her hands in her lap, folded them, and allowed an angelic expression to overtake her face.

Satisfied that the victory was hers, the mother went about her business browsing.

It is left to us to imagine just what kind of Jekyll/Hyde transformation the mother might have undergone had the girl defied her.

What, pray tell, is an "icky mama face"?

Obviously, this woman, perhaps without even realizing it, had mastered the once popular (1950s) maternal art of child control using face contortions.

It requires absolutely no hands-on component whatsoever.

The angered/frustrated/pained mother need only stare off a short distance past her child, tighten her lips, squint her eyes, and beam an expression geared to produce compliance in the troublemaker.

My mother was (in fact, still is) great at it. So accustomed have I become to it that I can tell when she is wearing the "icky mama face" while talking to me on the phone.

Her version of said face never fails to elicit the desired response. I give in.

I have tried using the "icky mama face" several times during my tenure as a mother, with less success.

Usually the troublemaker in question simply responds, "You're trying to lay a guilt trip on me, aren't you?"

Mrs. X Gets an Idea

Why is it fun being a grown-up?

Mrs. X lay in her bed and looked up at the ceiling. Her eyes were focused on a spiderweb crack in the plaster, right near the overhead light.

Even though she appeared to be concentrating on this defect, her mind was hundreds of miles away. It was in Canada.

Mrs. X knew she should get out of bed. She had a busy day and a long drive ahead of her. Still, she found it difficult to roust herself out from under the warm covers.

As she lay there, her thoughts left Canada and traveled, quite naturally, along that country's highways, across the bridge at Port Huron, Michigan, across and down the roads that led to down-state Michigan, up her driveway, through her living room, into her kitchen and back—far back—into her freezer.

They landed, finally, on the large rump roast she was keeping there under a thin layer of frost.

"Maybe I should get up and try to thaw that thing out," she said aloud to herself. And she tossed the blankets off her legs and stood up.

Mrs. X walked past the bedrooms of her sleeping children, glanced in to check on them and fumbled her way down the stairs to her kitchen.

The room was peaceful and clean, just as she had left it. Only the ticking of a wall clock disturbed the silence. Mrs. X stood for a moment with her hands in her robe pockets, and she appreciated the quiet.

She knew that it was just a matter of time before the calm would be broken by cries of, "When do we leave?" and "When do we eat?"

The roast had only partially thawed by noon, the hour when Mrs. X and her family planned to leave on their journey.

The four children, incredulous, gathered about her in the kitchen as she wrestled the grocer's packaging off the roast and replaced it with several layers of aluminum foil.

She rolled it and rolled it, as if she were wrapping a present, and patted the foil so it clung like wrinkled skin against the roast's sides.

50

"Do you really think it will bake?" her oldest daughter asked.

Her oldest daughter, though only nine, was a skeptic. She had seen Mrs. X cook and experiment with food before. This time, the girl had serious doubts.

Mrs. X had reached the point in her life where she no longer took offense at her children's judgments.

"Of course it will bake," she said, turning toward the garage door that was just off the kitchen.

Mrs. X asked one of her sons to open the door, and she gingerly stepped down the step before him, carrying the meat.

She set the roast on the roof of the car, got in the driver's seat and reached down to pull the latch that would unlock the hood. She pulled hard, straining a little, before she finally heard the hood release.

Mrs. X then got out of the car, lifted the hood so it was full open and retrieved the roast. Holding it off to one side, she peered around it into the cavern that held the automobile's machinery.

She recognized the spot where the dipstick was and she recognized, vaguely, the fan and the battery.

"You'll be surprised how much heat this engine will generate between here and Aunt Millie's," she said to her children.

Then, judging the flattest, most secure pocket of space she could find, she placed the roast alongside the engine and slammed down the hood.

"It should be cooked by the time we get there," she said.

She crossed her fingers inside a pocket where the children couldn't see.

"Now, on with the luggage," she said. And she walked back to unlock the trunk.

Mrs. X Cooks a Roast

Mom, what is your goal?

Mrs. X got into her car and placed her hands on the steering wheel. She looked at the wall of her garage and took a deep, relaxing breath.

"Now," she said, more to herself than the children who sat around her.

The children were eyeing one another suspiciously and were uncommonly quiet.

Mrs. X threw a look over her shoulder and, without turning on the car's ignition, pushed the clutch down as far as it would go. She felt the vehicle begin a slow roll onto the driveway.

Considering its angle, she knew the car could coast to the street without help from the engine. She planned to begin the cooking process from in front of her house and to begin it precisely on schedule.

As the car gradually picked up speed, she gave the steering wheel one hard turn to avoid a pothole and sighed with relief when it finally edged onto the road.

"Just a minute," Mrs. X said to her children as the car came to a stop. She pulled the lever that popped the car's hood and bolted out before they could begin their questions.

It seemed to them that Mrs. X had only just disappeared behind the open door when she climbed back into her seat.

"The roast hasn't budged one inch," she said proudly, and she glanced at her watch and turned the key in the ignition.

"Six hours alongside the hot engine should do it. It should be done by the time we reach Aunt Millie's."

Making the drive across Canada, Mrs. X found that she was frequently distracted from the task at hand. It was unnatural for her, but she imagined the worst kinds of thoughts.

What if one of the children had to use a rest room?

Mrs. X had sounded the bathroom alarm ("Does anybody have to go before we leave?") prior to boarding, but still she remained uneasy.

She feared that if she had to stop the car, the engine would cool enough to delay the roast's cooking. For a moment, she wished that she had thought to put a thermometer into the meat.

Then, out of nowhere, it occurred to her that a chicken or a whitefish might have been a better choice.

Considering this, Mrs. X was suddenly struck by an infinitely more miserable possibility.

What should she do if an animal tried to cross the road and she had to suddenly brake?

She was sure the roast would roll from its spot, fall down a wheel well and land, plop, under the car's rear tire.

Oh, horrors!

Mrs. X attempted to comfort herself by singing.

Mother said there'd be days like this, she began, and she was quickly silenced by her son, seated next to her, who said he was beginning to detect the scent of cooking meat coming through the vent.

Mrs. X was glad then that she had left the whitefish at home.

She looked nervously at her watch. Only two more hours to Aunt Millie's.

As it happened, Mrs. X's concerns were unfounded. She even felt vindicated when the family finally sat down to eat.

Looking at the moderately browned roast in the center of Aunt Millie's table, Mrs. X urged the children to offer up a prayer of thanksgiving.

She bowed her head, folded her hands and, unbeknownst to the others, crossed her fingers for the second time that day.

"Children," she said, when grace was finished. "I want you to savor this."

Where the Lost Things Go

How would you like to go money hunting?

Our old family couch preceded the blond furniture craze of the late 1950s.

Big, brown and lumpy, with slender threads coursing through it like veins, it seemed to me when I was a child to be a foreboding, if only sleeping, monster. And although it probably represented the height of fashion in its day, I thought it was ugly.

Who could know what horror lurked in the heart of such a beast? Or when it would show itself?

The fact that it sagged and smelled only lent credibility to my suspicions. But that was before we found the treasure hidden inside it.

Mother bought the couch just about the time I began to use my imagination, and she created a whole room around it with companion chairs and complimentary wallpaper. She liked to create rooms around things and once coerced Father into painting the kitchen walls the color of our parakeet's blue-green belly.

Mother showcased the couch by positioning it against the longest wall of the living room, where she referred to it, formally, as "The Davenport."

Using her own mysterious radar, she would say things like: "Don't bounce on The Davenport!" or "Get your shoes off The Davenport!" to my sister and me when we thought she wasn't looking.

There were some good things about the couch.

Its two plump cushions were soft, and my sister and I could stretch out full-length on them at the same time and not have to touch each other, which is important when you are young and siblings.

Other times, we cast off our differences and snuggled up together against the couch's big arm to watch scary movies, quite unaware that all the while we were sitting on a very special secret.

The day of discovery came in our early adolescence, when Mother decided the couch had served its purpose. That it had, perhaps, one lump too many and that a thorough cleaning was in order before it was banished to the dump. It was a rainy day and my sister and I groaned at the thought of helping her in her housework.

Mother began the work by removing the cushions and running her hand in the crack between the couch's back and its seat.

Amid the years' collection of dust and fuzz she found a single pair of scissors.

It was a triumph. She had discovered the first nugget in a vein of gold.

Encouraged, Mother, for the first time—and to our amazement—mounted the couch with her feet and trod the seat up and down. She widened its crack with her weight and happily bounced a little, giving the command for action: "Shove your hands down in there, girls, and see what else you can find!"

Formality had been given the heave-ho.

We went about our duty with a new and vigorous enthusiasm. And the couch, bursting with its load, yielded twelve pairs of scissors (Mother had hosted a sewing club), eleven combs, scads of pens and pencils, wooden and glass marbles, $2-plus in petty change, a Three Stooges ring, and a weather decoder given to me by Dale Meredith in the fifth grade.

The decoder showed blue, a prediction of rain under the cushions.

After the cleaning, the old couch went the way of doomed furniture. I have never seen its equal.

I confess, though, I do permit a bit of couch-bouncing in our household. Such an activity is good for the heart.

And I know, when some pleading voice cries, "Where's my . . . ?" just exactly where it is that the lost things go.

A Nose by Any Other Name Could Be a Popcorn Holder

Why is it we always buy popcorn, but we never eat it?

Mothering a toddler in your forties is not the same as mothering a toddler in your twenties. There is, I've learned firsthand, a certain calm and confidence that comes with age and experience.

By the time you're forty, you've pretty much got a grip on life and its little unexpected adventures—and that gives you an advantage.

You're smarter. You're more self-sufficient. And you don't tend to panic as much.

For example, if you've ever mothered before, you know that kids will get into poisonous cleansers and medicines if you leave them about, so you put them (the cleansers and medicines, that is) out of reach.

You understand that children thrive better when they are on some kind of schedule, so you eat regular meals and put them to bed at roughly the same time each night.

Of course, it is to be expected that you will, like your younger cohorts, have to deal with the flu or tonsillitis now and again.

And once in a while your darling will knock over a lamp or toss something precious down the toilet or use a cuss word.

But, because you are hardened to these little disturbances, you cheerfully cope. Thus, things run more smoothly in your life.

Still, no matter how well-prepared you think you are, that late-in-life baby will probably test your mettle at least once.

So it was that I found myself recently, on a Saturday night no less, dealing with the unexpected. I had tossed off all the things I normally do in a day, and I looked forward to a pleasant evening at home.

My mistake.

As a treat for after dinner, I prepared each child a bowl of popcorn and settled down to watch a movie with them.

I had no more than plopped my tired body onto a couch when my son, age four, approached me with a smile on his face.

Obviously, he was thrilled about something.

He spoke in a shy, soft voice that I could hardly hear at first. All I caught, initially, was a mumble about popcorn.

Silly me, I thought he wanted more.

"You want more already?" I asked him, displaying mock surprise.

He drew closer so I could hear him better. Nothing looked amiss. He spoke again.

"I put a popcorn up my nose," he said, gleefully.

"You did what?" I bellowed, bolting to my feet.

He turned away from me, poking a finger at his nose. I vaguely remember growling under my breath and stomping upstairs. I told The Perfectionist, who seemed unfazed and who turned back to his television program, and I then began a search for a magnifying glass and a flashlight.

Looking up a wiggling child's nose is not as easy as it sounds. And, supposing you do spot the lost object, seemingly miles away, a decision must then be made about how to retrieve it.

I had heard once from a friend, who is the daughter of a paramedic, that it is possible to suck a foreign body out of a nostril with your mouth.

This did not appeal to me.

I decided, instead, to pray for a sneeze and call the local after-hours clinic.

The doctor advised me to bring my son in. If left in the nose, a popcorn kernel can expand and create problems, he said.

I envisioned a popcorn plant growing out of my son's sinuses.

Once at the clinic, I mentioned my teenage daughters. They never cause me this kind of concern, I said in a dramatic huff to the doctor.

He laughed and I knew what he was thinking: Necessity is the mother of the $50 office call.

A Dream and a Wish

If you had a genie, what would you wish for?

One of the most vivid memories I have from my mentally retarded daughter's childhood has less to do with her mind than with my own.

She was five at the time of my particular memory, and although I had cared for her every day of those five years, I had not come to terms with her disabilities in that length of time.

During those years, despite her obvious limitations, a little gremlin living inside me pushed me into the hope that "normal" lay just beyond the next doctor's visit, or the next operation, or the next year's worth of physical therapy, or the next decade's worth of intensive schooling.

How I dreamed, as all mothers do, of the day when she would get a job, have her own apartment, drive her own car—indeed, cook her own meals, or even brush her own teeth.

My thinking was understandable, I guess, for the things that were amiss with her (and there are many) unraveled themselves over time, much like the layered skins of an onion.

I would just get an emotional handle on the reality that she had kidney problems, when I would have to face the fact that she had vision problems as well. Then I would adjust my thinking to accommodate her poor eyes, only to find out that she was losing her ability to walk . . . and so on through a long list of body functions. Along with my husband, I dealt as best I could with each crisis as it presented itself, and I fell ever more in love with her as she conquered these obstacles and challenges, one-by-one.

Frequently, she inspired me with her courage.

On the occasion of the aforementioned memory, she was but a little girl nestled in a car seat beside me, the size of a two-year-old toddler, unable to speak more than a few words and on her way to a hearing test.

As it happened, a bus loaded with mentally retarded adult residents from a neighboring group home pulled in front of our vehicle that day. As we drove along, my daughter gazed out the car window at the beautiful spring weather. And I, looking at the misshapen heads that bobbed aimlessly in the bus's window, gazed off into our future.

Then I wept for what I realized she could never be. For what I could not know. For what I was powerless to change.

And time passed.

Before I knew it, she was a young woman with a young woman's body and even some of a young woman's yearnings. Before I knew it, she was every bit of twenty-one years old.

One day, acting on the advice of doctors, I took her for her most recent in a lifetime of medical tests: A sleep study to determine whether she stops breathing in the night.

I walked her, arm-in-arm as we have grown accustomed to walking, into the familiar setting of a hospital, and she carried with her, tucked under her free arm as she has for every hospital visit, her beloved Cabbage Patch doll, Ethel.

She learned a long time ago that Ethel has powers to keep her fears at bay. And no amount of growing up is ever going to change that.

I sat on the bed that doubled as a technician's lab and watched while yet another stranger hooked my daughter up to a series of machines that would monitor her breathing, her brain waves, her heartbeats, her pulse rhythms.

I sat with the technician into the wee hours of morning, watching with him as he observed her on a television screen, evaluating the signals that came from her body. We watched while she cuddled Ethel innocently in her sleep.

The technician told me, after observing her all night, that my daughter is a restless sleeper who awakens frequently, and that she spends very little time in the rapid eye movement—or REM—stage of sleep.

That means she spends very little time dreaming.

It is not surprising.

Somewhere along the line—and I could not tell you when that was—I took over the task of dreaming on her behalf. That task has kept me up nights, too.

Trying It On for Size

Can you spin on the heel of your shoe?

Used to be when my son was three, I could keep an eye on him with my ears. That is to say I could locate him and monitor his activities just by listening.

Loud cackles coming from the living room told me he was playing witch. Rhythmic thumps rolling down the hallway let me know he was jumping on his bed. The sound of plastic on rubber said he was in his bedroom, and his swords were out of their box.

One morning I couldn't hear anything. I began an anxious search. He wasn't in the living room. He wasn't in the kitchen. He wasn't down in the family room.

Finally, almost sensing his presence, I zeroed in on him in his older sister's room. He wasn't supposed to play there without permission. It was home to an assortment of tempting items that could get him into trouble. Blocks to swallow. Records to break. Drawers to rummage through.

I approached the door as quietly as possible and opened it a crack to peek in. I was full of curiosity, relieved that I had found him, certain that I would catch him in some mischievous act.

I expected him to pause in mid-trouble, his wide brown eyes looking at me with a suggestion of guilt.

Instead, what I saw made my heart skip.

He was on the floor concentrating, quietly trying to get his sister's leg brace onto his bare, knobby leg.

He had stretched his leg out to full length, and he had it inside the straps. His fingers were working furiously to tighten them down. Miles away from his wriggling toes, the brace's ugly brown shoe pointed vacantly up toward the ceiling. He was totally unaware of my presence.

The brace—a long, battered, stiff appliance of steel and leather— keeps my daughter out of a wheelchair. It is as much a part of our household as the television, washing machine and car.

My daughter has worn a brace for over ten years. She took to it happily, even proudly, from the outset. She knew, as my husband and I did, that it would make all the difference in her quality of life.

It never occurred to us when our son was born several years into that life, that he would need an explanation about why she has to wear one.

I watched him that day, attempting to understand in his own way, I suppose, why her life is different from his.

He put the brace on. He sat in it for a while. He looked at it and touched, admiringly, the few places where the metal still shined.

Finally, after a long spell, he eased his leg out, stood up, spotted me in the doorway and scampered over for a hug.

Without missing a beat, he hurried on to another adventure.

I stayed in the doorway and watched him run down the hall. His back was straight. His elbows pumped and his hair stood up with the breeze his running created.

Behind him, the brace lay important, but lifeless, of course.

My Problem Now

What is a mile?

This year, for the first time in years, we may be able to get both our vehicles in our two-car garage.

That's because over the summer, I finally moved a half of a bedroom set out of the garage and into the basement, where it belongs.

Soon, I guess, I will have to move my daughter's big bicycle down there too. Too bad. It really deserves to winter in a showplace.

That bike represents the courage of a little girl.

It's been so long now that I don't really remember when it was that my daughter finally learned to pedal. She didn't walk until she was three or so. Probably didn't pedal until she was somewhere between five and seven years old.

Back then, I bought her one of those low-slung three-wheelers so she wouldn't have far to fall.

She tooled around the circle in front of our house on that bike until her slow-growing body was finally too big for it, with time out for the four years in the late 1980s when her left leg quit working.

This past summer, she went out to ride it again, and I watched while she awkwardly eased her now-adult frame onto that little three-wheeler. It was dirty and scratched, and the Strawberry Shortcake doll emblems had worn off.

None of that concerned her.

I watched while she tried to pedal. There was no room for her legs to turn. She would be content to just sit.

Finally, I decided it was time to buy her a new bike, and I told her so.

I don't think she really understood what I was trying to convey: A new bike would accommodate her size better. And we would get one with three wheels. I still didn't want her to fall.

So it was that on a dreary rainy day last June, I drove her to a local bicycle dealer. Her eyes grew wide when we entered the showroom and she saw the array of options. Colors galore. Mountain bikes. Training bikes. Stationary bikes. Racing bikes.

What to choose?

What my daughter didn't know was that I had ordered her a red, adult three-wheeler especially built for disabled riders.

A clerk wheeled it out to her, and suddenly the hum of business that pervaded the store was gone.

All eyes, those of employees and customers, alike, looked to my daughter, each of them delighting in what may have been the most wonderful moment in her life.

"Wow!" she exclaimed, her eyes huge. "Do I get to keep it forever?"

She stroked it like a proud owner would caress a pet.

One trip around the circle-shaped street in front of our home was all she got before the sky opened up, and we were forced to put the bike away.

At dinnertime, I found her in the garage, staring at it appreciatively.

My guess is she never considered all she had been through preceding that glorious purchase: Two serious operations, in which there was a threat that she could lose her leg completely. Months in casts. Leg braces. Years of physical therapy that made her scream in pain.

My problem now is that she wants to ride the bike down the street by herself. Soon she will want to tour the neighborhood alone.

My mind tells me this would be good for her. Unfortunately, my heart doesn't want to let her go.

The Gift

What do you mean by compassion?

*"I am send symbol of God. A piece of bread. We all
want peace in the world."* —Krystyna Szczygtowska

I have had in my dresser drawer, for over a year now, a
communion wafer from Poland. It is large by American standards
and is rectangular in shape.

On one side it is embossed with figures of the Three Wise Men
worshipping the infant Jesus, who is resting in his mother Mary's
arms. Over them, the Christmas star shines. And to their left, a tiny
corner of the wafer is missing, though not from a bite.

Krystyna sent it to me with a message of love several Christmases
ago. It is easily one of the most beautiful gifts I have ever received.

I have no idea where she got it.

Krystyna and I met many summers ago while our daughters, both
handicapped, were undergoing medical treatment at a Shriners
hospital.

She spoke very little English and carried with her a Polish-to-
English dictionary, which she turned to frequently for help.

Her large, dark eyes, however, said what her lips could not: She
was alone. A little scared. A lot hopeful—putting much of her
child's future and well-being into the hands of American strangers
who were volunteering their care.

I spoke no Polish whatsoever and yet, with smiles, gestures,
tentative glances and that dictionary, we were able to strike up a
friendship.

She told me about her sparse and tiny apartment in Poland, the
two small daughters and husband that she had left behind, as well as
her job at an airport, and how she commuted about her home city
on a bicycle.

One day I decided I would take her with me to visit the local
Toys R Us, as I had a car with me and thought perhaps she would
like a chance to get away from the hospital.

She got into my car and was filled with amazement. What were all the knobs for? How do you put on a seat belt? How do you get yourself out?

It is difficult to explain the mixed feelings I had as we walked into the enormous store.

I was filled with pride for our people and for what we have achieved in our short history. At the same time, I felt a twinge of embarrassment.

The sheer wealth and plenty of our nation was manifest across Krystyna's face.

Shopping at the toy store with Krystyna was like no shopping experience I have ever had. She had to look at and touch every marvelous toy on every towering shelf.

She put her fingers tentatively on dolls and blocks and books and paints and cars and stuffed animals and games and then she put them, just barely, to her lips.

Where to begin!

She muttered to me that there was nothing comparable in her country and said that many of the toys we buy for about $20 here would sell for nearly $100 in Poland—if they were ever made available.

I knew before we went, but she did not, that I would buy her daughters a toy before we left the store.

Tears welled up in both our eyes as we settled on a Fisher Price dollhouse with little people. They would make her children the envy of their neighborhood, Krystyna said.

Six months later the "piece of bread" arrived in the mail.

It is so easy to know who gave the greater gift.

Mrs. X Surprises the Congregation

What is the most amazing thing your imagination can think of?

I never met Mrs. X, but I have a lot of sympathy for her predicament.

What could have been more stressful than being a 1960s mother pressed for time, with a last-minute marketing decision to make, on a Sunday morning when most stores were closed?

Imagine:

Secretly, Mrs. X wanted to roll over and go back to sleep. She even let herself shut off the alarm, and she dozed for a few minutes before awakening with a start.

Drat! She was late.

Mrs. X threw back the covers and moved from the warmth of her bed with a suddenness that surprised her aching bones.

She stood for a moment, letting them adjust, and then scratched herself and shuffled her way into the bathroom.

The face in the mirror was hers.

She looked at it closely and pulled on her cheeks to stretch away the wrinkles and remind herself of the beauty that once was. Then she splashed it with water.

Mrs. X went to awaken her children—she joked silently with herself that she would scare them—with her rollers still wound into her hair.

They were bristle rollers that she had owned forever, and she had placed them in neat rows going backward from her face.

This morning the rollers were askew from sleep, and their pink picks stuck out in every direction.

Nevertheless, Mrs. X left them on her head until the very last minute. She wanted their curls to keep through the church service and the fellowship hour that followed.

Mrs. X was never really sure whether it was better to have her children get dressed for church and then eat—and hope they missed spilling something on their clean clothes—or to have them eat and then have them get dressed.

Usually when she followed the latter inclination they changed their minds about what to wear too many times. And they dawdled.

During the week, Mrs. X usually put two or three cold cereal choices and some bread for toast on the table for breakfast. But on Sundays, she always asked her children what they wanted to eat because she believed Sundays were special.

A lot of times they chose scrambled eggs and juice. Simple.

It seemed to Mrs. X, however, that whenever she was running late they asked for pancakes and bacon.

On this morning, the children, still sleepy-eyed and somewhat cranky, didn't disappoint her.

She figured she lost a good forty-five minutes breaking up spats, mixing batter, forming pancakes and dispensing them to four hungry mouths. Then she lost another ten minutes doing dishes and washing syrup off the table and the children's hands before sending them off to fetch their clothes.

Miraculously, after sounding the bathroom alarm ("Does anybody have to go before we leave?"), Mrs. X managed to get out of the house with the children and her hairdo intact—and with just enough time to beat the choir procession down the aisle.

When she got to the church, her pastor greeted her at the door, smiling and talking under his breath.

"We've nearly run out of juice for communion. Could you run and get some more?" he asked her.

Mrs. X didn't know how to tell her pastor no.

She felt stressed but bundled her children back into the car and left in search of an open market.

She passed three that were closed before she remembered one on the other side of town that served customers seven days a week. It would be faster to make a beeline there than to drive aimlessly looking, she thought. And she was right.

Unfortunately, when she got there, the market was out of the necessary grape juice.

Mrs. X reacted.

She leaned across the counter, exasperated, and looked the proprietor in the eyes.

"Where's the prune juice?" she asked.

Motherjokes

Do you know how hot Venus is?

The great thing about small children is that they view the world wondrously and with imagination.

To them, everything is exciting and new. There is nothing more curious than a snowflake or rainbow, and few things are as thought-provoking as a hill of busy ants.

What might seem to be the most mundane activity to adults can appear fabulous in children's eyes.

Or, as I learned recently while trying to add spice to our February existence, horrifying.

My son, age six, feared the worst when I walked into the living room wearing my new swimming goggles last week.

I figured as long as I was going to try them on for size, I might as well show him how I looked.

You know, tease him a little, get a reaction, let him see the lighter side of Mom.

He'll get a laugh out of this, I told myself, guessing that he would want me to do something spontaneous and out of the ordinary.

I slipped the goggles on in the bathroom, adjusted them before the mirror (wow, did they fit tight!), made a face at myself and moved into the hallway.

My hair, freshly cut, was sticking out at all angles from the wide rubber band that held the goggles to my head. They were flat against my face. My cheeks, brow and ears pooched out around them, red.

Creeping toward the living room, I called his name and leaned forward, around a wall, deliberately looming at him.

"How do I look?" I asked, grinning broadly. "Do I look silly?"

He turned away from the television program he was watching, with his tongue poking at his inside cheek, and he examined me with a sober face. His back was erect, his eyes were wide and his eyebrows were seriously creased.

"No," he said in response to my questions, putting his hands on his hips, dramatically.

He paused for effect.

"You're not going to wear those to the puppet show tomorrow, are you?" he asked.

Huh?

I ripped the goggles off my head, pulling a few hairs with them, then turned around and stomped back toward the bathroom.

What, I asked myself, did I ever do to that boy that would cause him to have such a thought?

Why would he imagine that I would take him to the library puppet show wearing a pair of swimming goggles?

I can hardly wait until he's about fourteen years old. He'll be ripe for some serious teasing about then.

My oldest daughter was that age when he was born.

Let me tell you, there's nothing more humiliating when you're in junior high school than a mother who wears maternity clothes.

If you were to ask her, my daughter would probably tell you that she wished I had goggles back then.

Big ones.

Mrs. X Accepts a Challenge

Is being a contortionist a bad thing?

Mrs. X was on her last child (and he was halfway grown) before she began to really appreciate the ritual of tucking a child into bed. She could not account for the thought's timing, but she realized one night that with this boy—now almost into his teen years—she would one day soon have to give up the practice for good.

For a moment, the thought made her insides weep.

As with carving pumpkins, or car-pooling, or packing school lunches, Mrs. X had been doing this task with one child or another for more than twenty years. And with each child that she had helped to slip into a world of dreams, she had performed the ritual in the same three-step pattern.

It was a pattern that she could do with her eyes closed: A question about how the day had gone. A prayer that included all relatives, friends and pets. A kiss to the just-this-side-of-clean forehead.

(So accomplished was she that she could, indeed, plant her kisses directly on her restless targets without having to search them out with a light.)

Over time, Mrs. X had learned that most days went well. And that most prayers were answered. And that most slightly-dirty foreheads carried a taste of salt.

Standing with her son at his bed this evening, Mrs. X realized with a start that the top of his head now reached nearly to her chin. For a moment, she concentrated on his features: the dark, deep-set eyes that he owed to his father and the red tints in his hair that harked back to her side of the family. It amazed her to think that not all that long ago the boy had fit comfortably on her lap.

Mrs. X knew he would never settle there again.

"Time for you to hit the sack," she said to him, using a tuck-in phrase that had been handed down through her female family members for who-knows-how-many generations.

She wondered what the phrase "hit the sack" actually meant in its heyday. And she leaned forward slightly and rolled back the boy's blankets as she thought.

He watched her hands tugging gently.

"There's one thing I can do that the other kids can't do," her son said to her, and he got her attention, and she lifted her head.

Mrs. X knew her son longed to outshine the others, just once. She also knew how hard that could be.

"Really? What's that?" she asked and she looked into his face, wondering what he would have to say.

Mrs. X guessed that the boy could sing a very high note, or that he could read faster than his classmates, or that he could build a card pyramid higher than anyone else.

The boy looked back at her hard and earnestly, and he spoke with a conviction that she imagined would become even stronger with manhood.

It was a conviction that she hoped he would use to right wrongs when he became an adult.

"Put my whole fist into my mouth," is what the boy said.

Mrs. X heard her voice go out into the night air and turn a phrase from the 1990s.

"No way," she said, slanting her upper body backward for effect, and before she knew it she had added an emphatic, "Prove it."

And so he did.

Mrs. X watched incredulously while the boy opened his mouth as far as it would go—showing his back molars and his tonsils—and while he rolled his long fingers into tight balls and pushed them completely, thumb and pinkie knuckles following the middle ones, over his lips.

He turned toward her and addressed her as a soldier addresses his officer, and he waited for her reaction, the stuffed hand mocking a salute.

Mrs. X then hauled out a phrase she remembered from the 1960s. "Oh, gross!" she wailed, and then she quickly put a finger to her lips and said "shh" to no one in particular. She was afraid that their conversation would awaken the slumbering household.

Mrs. X thought back to the time when the boy had entertained the Sunday school class by carrying a quarter between his two front teeth, and for just a moment she allowed herself to marvel at his peculiar form of genius.

"Can you put your fist in your mouth?" the boy asked her, swiping his wet fingers across his pajamas.

Mrs. X said, no, she couldn't, and she hurried through her prayer, and she planted her kiss, and she omitted her question about how the day had gone.

On her way out of his bedroom, with the satisfied boy nestling in his bed behind her, Mrs. X dared to sneak a fist up to her lips.

She opened her mouth as wide as she could and urged two big knuckles against the tips of her teeth.

The teeth made her knuckles hurt but not as much as that night's realization.

A mother can have only so many children, she knew.

And a boy can only be a child for just so long.

Coming Home

Did you know Dad before you married him?

We had walked the sidewalks lining Main Street so many times before. I with my dreams. He with his wide, steady stride and straight forward gaze, listening as I spoke of my contentment.

"This village is home," I told him often.

This had been my favorite grandparents' village. The place where they had worked and sang, prayed and loved the land. Where they'd loved their children and their children's children.

At the end of this very Main Street their old farmhouse stood, inviting me still, though my grandparents were long dead.

In coming to their village to live, I felt a family cycle had been completed.

On this evening, we were silent as we walked, each intent on our destination, the somber shades of nighttime coming down about us.

Deep in thought, he was preparing his mind to face that which he had not faced for twenty-one years. It was not easy for him to concentrate, for we had argued and he was still angry. At himself.

At me.

In his frustration he had lashed out at me: "Have you got the guts to face the truth?" he asked.

This dark side of him made me feel most uncomfortable. Pacing myself beside him, I longed to reach out and grasp one of his hands, but he had them shoved deep into his pockets.

Instead, I crossed my arms in front of my chest and gulped down breaths to keep my tears at bay.

Ahead of us, in a cafe, a young man waited.

m   m   m

I took the initiative, pulling wide the heavy wooden door and stepping into the dim, candle-lit dining room. He followed close. We were, he told the hostess, here to meet a third party. The hostess took the young man's name when he was unable to provide a description.

Seated, we looked nervously at one another before he asked me, "How will I know him?"

He scanned the room with his eyes: The young and old men at the bar. The white-haired ladies struggling to divide their dinner costs fairly. The lovers sipping wine and cooing.

I held my answer for a time.

"That's him over there," I finally said, rolling my eyes toward a lone figure at a table for four near the rear exit. I had found him almost immediately. To me, the young man stood conspicuously out from the crowd, as if he wore a sign across his forehead that proclaimed his identity.

"What makes you so sure?" he asked, anxiously following my gaze across the room. The young man was sitting stiffly with his hands wrapped tightly around a glass. His eyes focused steadily on the front door through which we had just come.

I was certain.

Even in the dim light I recognized his features. The wide nose. The long upper lip. The heavy, arched eyebrows. The sad, longing eyes.

"That's him," I insisted, saying at last what needed to be said. "He is your son."

We waited uncomfortably, trying not to stare, making small talk while the young man raised and lowered his glass to and from his lips, sipping slowly.

At long last he arose and joined us at our table.

m   m   m

For the first time in our married years, I realized with a jolt just how old and tired my husband looked. His cheeks were sunken along the jaw line. Deep, permanent circles were etched beneath his eyes.

For one fleeting, confusing moment, it seemed to me that the young man so much resembled the groom that I remembered, that he should have been my husband. He had the smooth skin, the thick brown hair, the steady, slender hands—the hope.

The balding, nervous man seated beside me seemed the stranger. It occurred to me that, despite our many years together, I had never really known my own mate.

My husband stood and extended his right hand, as if he didn't know what else to do. I knew that he would never spontaneously embrace the young man, and wondered what the young man was expecting.

He grasped my husband's hand firmly but did not speak. He nodded ever so subtly, as if to reassure himself that the specter of a long-cherished vision had finally materialized.

I noticed that his eyes, new to me yet so familiar, were brimming with tears. To me, he seemed just a boy and, despite his adult figure, that was the way I would always remember him.

Just One Day

Have you ever heard the saying, "My heart feels heavy?"

Right now, as I write this, three tiny babies, born more than three months prematurely to a friend of mine, are struggling to hold on to their lives.

Their brother, the fourth of the quadruplets, died last night after a two-week fight that involved a lot of machines and doctors and prayers.

While he was dying, I was having a dream.

In the dream, I was embracing my friend, crying with her and sharing her pain, as if that were possible. We were hurrying to find answers to impossible questions in buildings of my mind's creation, and placing phone calls to doctors without faces.

Occasionally, throughout the dream, I would change places with my friend.

When I awoke, the pain from the dream was as real and as raw as that of a fresh stab wound.

Time, I decided with a start, still sitting on the edge of my bed, does not heal all wounds like the old adage says.

It merely covers them up.

Twenty-one years ago, I was where my friend is today: grieving and making funeral arrangements for a baby. A baby who lived just one day.

After my son's death, I did what most grieving parents do. I tried not to, but I questioned God. I asked "why" a thousand times.

I questioned doctors. "What could we have done differently?"

And I questioned myself. "What did I or didn't I do?"

Eventually, I began to think about the meaning of life—and its purpose—especially in the context of just one day.

What, I asked myself, is the significance of a single day in time? What can be accomplished in that brief span? What can be dreamed of? Hoped for? Felt?

Why, I wondered, would a baby be allowed just one day? Enough time to get thirsty and hungry, but not enough time to feast on the pleasures of life.

The hospital rules in existence all those years ago allowed him no more than the clinical touches of strangers and an opportunity for baptism.

Watching the baptism from behind a window, tears streaming down my face, I wondered if my son could sense the love my husband and I were sending him.

I learned a lot from that experience.

Trust me when I tell you that each and every life, no matter its length nor its particulars, is truly a precious gift.

And so is each and every day. Even the ones that break your heart.

A Visit from the Iceman

I wonder why we have a sense of sad?

I step out into a dark and frozen world. The Iceman has been here on an overnight visit, and everything around me glistens in the frozen yet strangely beautiful painting he has left behind.

I enter that painting with a delicately placed step off my front porch and inch my way to the newspaper box, trying not to fall.

Reaching my destination safely, I anchor myself to the box's post and pause to take in the scene that is my neighborhood.

It is quiet and black.

Next door, a garage light that activates with a sensor is frozen on. It, and the perpetually burning bedroom light of another neighbor, give the painting what little color it has: a touch of yellow.

I am sure that the people next door are asleep. The children who live there tire themselves completely, as children do. And usually, they tire their parents as well.

Sleep falls across them easily, as Nature intended.

I am less certain about activities at the other neighbor's house. There, night and day, noon and midnight, merge into one long existence, and sleep does not come easily.

The woman who lives there stays in her bed twenty-four hours a day. She wishes. She prays. She remembers. She cries.

Pictures of her three children—the reasons she struggles for life— are posted on a board next to her shoulders. The two youngest, minors, visit her in spurts and starts—whenever their father cares to bring them. The oldest comes when his emotions allow.

I suspect, as I gaze at her light in these early morning hours, that my neighbor is being comforted by her television.

The Iceman has visited her personally.

From the waist down, she is as frozen and as twisted (she would tell you this herself) as the ice-weighted limbs of the trees.

Many of the terrible things that can happen to a person have happened to her. She is crippled by multiple sclerosis. Her parents, who used to help her, have died. And her only brother has written her off as a burden.

Her husband has divorced her and taken their children, and she is financially troubled.

She is lonely.

Recently, doctors advised her that she should have her legs amputated.

How, I wonder, can she bear to lose anything more? How can she even contemplate such a decision?

Still anchored to the newspaper post, I loose my grip and take a well-placed step toward my house. Moving through the painting, I take a last glance at her burning light and think back to a conversation she and I had this week.

"You've got to live life," she said to me with a smile.

And I am out here doing it, like all of us, I realize, on very slippery ground.

Cleopatra in the Dark

Does everybody die?

She tilts her head back and opens her mouth to receive the red grape I am dangling above her.

She is black-haired and fair-skinned, and I call her Cleopatra, joking that she is the object of royal attention.

My little tease breaks the strain that fills her room, and I begin to feed her, awkwardly.

I am surprised by the intimacy of this act.

Feeding an adult is strangely personal and unnatural. It is not the same as feeding an infant. There is trust but no cuddling. And there are smiles but no real happiness.

Outside, night has come. Her room is dark except for the light provided by her television and a flashing VCR clock that is stuck on 12:00.

She wants the lights out, and I leave them so. Reality is not as harsh in black and white.

I seat myself beside her bed and scoop food onto a fork, making sure that I vary the selections, and I deposit it as neatly as possible on her tongue.

She accepts my offerings with the eagerness of a baby bird, and she is grateful.

I notice that she chews with her mouth shut. She has good manners, I tell myself. And I scoop again. Soon we fall into a rhythm.

It has been months, maybe even a full year, since she has been out of her bedroom.

The closets, which stretch the length of an entire wall, gape at her, their doors long gone. They are filled with dresses and robes that date back to when she was a teen some twenty years ago.

She has no use for them now, but her daughter likes to wear them when she comes to visit, she tells me, adding wistfully, "They say if you save something long enough . . . ."

Aside from her television, which is standing on a bureau opposite her bed, all her other necessities—mostly pills and glasses full of water—are within arm's reach.

One arm's reach is all she is capable of.

Her fragile, twisted body, wracked by multiple sclerosis, has been robbed of most of its mobility.

But she can think clearly. As clearly as ever, except when emotions overcome her.

On this night, I wonder if her emotions have clouded her judgment, and I dare to ask her if she has ever considered entering a nursing home.

She is as aware as I am that she needs nursing care.

She laughs uncomfortably and tells me she spent twenty-two days in a nursing home once.

I ask her, point-blank, if that experience was worse than being alone twenty-four hours a day, bedridden, with nothing but her thoughts.

She has a bite of tuna salad in her mouth, and her face contorts around it as tears come.

"I will commit suicide before I will go into another one," she tells me, looking deep into my face.

It is that possibility, an arm's length away, that frightens me.

The Passing

Do birds go in boxes when they die?

It happened to be a beautiful Friday, just at the end of twilight. The sun was making its final descent in a splash of pinks, and there were just enough rolling clouds to make the sky seem alive.

They moved over our truck and brought darkness with them and, maybe, made full night come a little bit early.

My son and I watched from our windows while three planes came out of that sky to land at the local airport as we were driving by.

My son always marvels at the miracle of flight.

The car in front of ours was a junker. Four heads bobbed around inside of it when it bounced over potholes. The four heads turned to face one another frequently, and they leaned in close to one another and fell back in laughter as well.

Four heads out for fun on a Friday night.

It is possible the driver of the junker was so busy bobbing and laughing that he didn't see the ducks in the road.

He slammed his brakes on long enough to make a short, screeching sound come out of his tires . . . and then he was gone, leaving behind three bewildered ducks, one of which was injured.

I stopped my truck and got out.

The injured duck was a male mallard. It sat in the road surrounded by its own feathers, and it watched the long row of cars that by now had slowed to a crawl.

I expect that it would have cried if it could have. A single, orange leg jutted out straight from its side and a patch of raw flesh, featherless, oozed onto the pavement.

I bent over and scooped the duck up. It was as light as a sponge.

What do you do with an armload of duck?

I got back into our truck, urged my son over and placed the duck between us on the seat, wrapped in my son's beach towel.

I stroked its lovely head, gently, and it watched while I shifted into first gear and eased the truck back onto the road.

My son said, "I have always wanted a duck."

It only took the duck a few minutes to die. It sat silently in the truck, then it laid its head down and gave one last, good stretch of its wings.

Then it was gone.

My son had never seen anything die before. I thought he would cry.

He didn't.

Instead, he asked me, after the duck's last breath, why it didn't go immediately to heaven.

I had to get into the specifics of souls and bodies and burials.

It was completely dark when we got home.

I came into the house and rummaged around in my oldest daughter's closet for a shoe box.

I found one that carried the label, "Birkenstock," and I pulled out her sandals, and I tucked the duck inside. My son helped me dig a hole in the dark that night.

The First Walker Theorem of Motherly Confusion

Mom, have you ever spotted something weird going on in your life?

The First Walker Theorem of Motherly Confusion states that a woman on laundry day, having lost enough sleep, will become addled in direct proportion to the number of years she has had offspring (who change their clothes at least three times a day) living in the home.

Similarly, its corollary states that a husband—supposing he is a perfectionist inclined to preach and that he preceded the children—can be considered responsible. It is that corollary with which we are concerned today.

I offer the following case study, which I call, "A Wet $20 Bill Is More Beautiful Than A Wet Light Bulb" as evidence. To wit:

Only last week, on an otherwise dull morning, I opened the washing machine to find a cool, clean $20 bill peeking up at me from a wet blouse.

I was thrilled.

I snatched it up, wrung it out a little, shook it, fluffed it, and looked around to make sure no one was watching. I then carried it tenderly upstairs to my dresser drawer, where I hid it, hoping it would dry.

Oh, the visions of shopping I enjoyed that morning!

By coincidence, The Perfectionist asked me over dinner that night, "What happened to this week's paycheck?"

Knowing the twenty dollars hadn't come from the check (the laundry pile was about ten days old and predated payday) and fearing a lecture about the merits of searching pockets before laundering clothing, I said quite truthfully, but with a smile, "I spent it on groceries and gasoline."

I might have told him about the find had I not remembered, in a flash, a drama-in-wifedom in which my sister once found herself.

It went something like this: On an ordinary day (You know the kind. The dog gets loose. The toilet plugs. At least one child has the flu.), she happened to lift her washing machine lid to find a well-laundered, still-intact light bulb.

Only the ghosts-of-pockets-past knew how it got there.

Unfortunately, her husband, who doesn't believe in ghosts, was standing by her side when the unveiling took place, and he was ready to pounce.

The light bulb could have disintegrated into thousands of pieces, cutting the family for months to come each time they got dressed, he said, using words to that effect.

It could have plugged the machine's drain pipe. It could have made its way into a sock, become stuck on the back of a dress shirt and, if enough static electricity was generated in the dryer, made him glow throughout the workday.

Today, she gives thanks that he wasn't present the time she washed one of his bullets.

Can you imagine the headlines (let alone the scene) that situation might have caused: *Woman Uses Rinse Cycle To Shoot Husband*—or—*"I Didn't Know The Machine Was Loaded" Woman Cries At Preliminary Hearing.*

Doing the laundry, it would seem, can be a lot like playing with a giant jack-in-the-box. The thrill comes in popping the lid.

Mrs. X Barks Back

You've tasted your socks?

Mrs. X one day wondered what it would be like to bark away her boredom. She wondered this while she stooped over a pile of neglected laundry that was cluttering her basement floor.

A red sock poked out of the pile, taunting her the way a child's out-thrust tongue might. "Nah-nah, nah-nah, nah-nah. You've got to do the laundry," she imagined the sock chanting.

Mrs. X kicked the sock and then gathered it with a big armful of dirty cast-off shirts and promptly threw them into the washing machine. She gave the *on* button a forceful twist and turned to lean against her dryer, pausing with a modicum of satisfaction while water swept in to drown out the sock.

Outside, she could hear her dog going through its familiar, monotonous, deliberate woof-woof-woofs.

"There must be a leaf passing over the sidewalk," she said to the always patient dryer.

Some days, Mrs. X stood covertly behind her closed basement door and watched through its narrow window while the dog barked with his back toward her. It seemed to her as if the dog never barked at anything important. It barked at the breeze. It barked when her neighbor went out to collect his newspaper. It barked when birds landed on the telephone wires.

Mrs. X hated to admit it, but she had wondered why she had given in to her children's pressures to buy a dog.

They would play with it, they promised her. They would feed it and give it water. They would clean its kennel and scoop the yard. "Oh, please, please, please, can't we have one?" they had begged.

Mrs. X listened hard over the drone of the washing machine, while the pitch of the dog's voice went up a few octaves. It barked furiously now, over and over. She was sure the overfed Siamese from three doors down was scouting mice in her yard. The dog would bark as long as the cat tempted him, she knew.

Envious of the dog's energy and endurance, Mrs. X wondered if, deep down inside, she secretly possessed a capacity like the dog's. A capacity to go on and on against the mundane.

She pressed herself harder against the dryer and turned her face toward the basement ceiling.

She was alone—the sock/tongue now making its way through the rinse cycle.

A rush went up her spine.

"Row-row-row," Mrs. X said, almost modestly, in a very low voice, mimicking the dog.

It felt good.

"Woof," she said, encouraged, and she summoned a growl. "Arf-arf."

Mrs. X aimed her face at what was left of the laundry pile. She cocked her head and gave one last, forceful bark before she turned to ascend the stairs.

Fleetingly, Mrs. X thought she saw the laundry cower. When she described her day to her family that night, they suggested to her that maybe she needed to take up a hobby.

Mrs. X thought then that she might try baying at the moon.

Cat Scratch Fever?

Do you know what I think would be really weird?

Not so very long ago, a local veterinarian stroked my cat's beautiful pewter-colored fur and announced that I was lucky he had some personality. (The cat, not the veterinarian, that is.)

Gray cats, this vet said, are usually blah.

I remember looking back at him and sending a silent "thank you" heavenward even as the vet was completing his examination.

There are very few things I dislike in life more than a blah cat.

Nevertheless, I wondered at the time: "What in the world does a cat's color have to do with his personality?"

For me, there was a link missing in the common-sense portion of our conversation.

(There was also a fear there. Having gone gray myself, I wondered if the same rationale could be applied to me. Is my personality dependent on my hair coloring? Did my personality change when I went from brown to gray? Have I been blaming my hormones for what my hair did? What if I were bald or wore a wig?)

(Then I had a second thought: What kind of personality would one of those patchy, tricolor calico cats have? Or, worse yet, a striped cat? Soon, I realized my thoughts were getting away from me, and I quit thinking. Period.)

I let the matter drop until one afternoon when my oldest daughter and I sat down to have a leisurely and much needed conversation.

There we were at the dining room table, happily launched into a discussion of some interest, when along came the cat, skulking by with his nose in the air, his tail curved into a modified question mark, his green eyes seeking out a paper grocery bag that rested against a nearby kitchen wall.

"Today I," began my daughter as a rhythmic, sort of irritating sandpaper-on-wood sound came into the room.

"Today I," she said louder, in an attempt to be heard.

The sandpaper sound continued, and we looked across the kitchen countertop to see the cat—sitting upright on his haunches, his hooded eyes focused intently as he vigorously and deliberately beat his front paws, one after the other, on the paper bag.

The bag would cave in a little with each pawing and then rebound to its original shape, only to be hit again.

We watched for a while and then, finally, after her amazement had begun to wear off, my daughter asked with some not-too-well-disguised curiosity, "What is he doing?"

She diverted our conversation with a measure of abruptness.

I looked at my daughter and I said, plainly, "He's beating the bag."

"Does he do that often?" she replied.

Actually, the cat does beat the bag fairly often, but he didn't commence this activity until he was well into his adulthood.

The beating of the bag is a deliberate act on his part. It always occurs in the late afternoon, but before evening and, interestingly enough, never on a weekend. Typically, it occurs when I am trying to have a conversation with an adult family member—usually The Perfectionist—but not always.

Now this is where the scenario I have laid out for you gets especially (forgive me) hairy. The real question should be: Why does the cat beat the bag?

Based on the veterinarian's hypothesis, I feel comfortable concluding that the beating of the bag—and maybe even the urge to do so—somehow accompanies a stressed-out lifestyle.

I have a certain personal reason for my thinking. (Though heaven only knows what is troubling our overfed and lazy cat; he has never wrecked the car, lost a spoon down the disposal, over-drawn the checking account or, for that matter, thrown a birthday party for twenty little girls.)

Anyway, the fact is, I sometimes get the urge to beat the bag myself. To remove the frozen vegetables and meats and eggs and butter and milk and to just pound away to my heart's content.

"Paper or plastic?" the bag boys ask me as they catch me staring off into space from the grocery line.

"Paper," I reply and I smile innocently and tell myself on the drive home that beating the bag is what keeps my cat from climbing the walls.

Seems like it could do as much for me.

I Run Over It (Once)

(with a nod to William Shakespeare)

Why are we going in circles?

"I have been in such a pickle since I saw you last." —*The Tempest*,
Act 5, Scene 1

How long were the mud flaps missing from the car before The Perfectionist noticed? A month? Two? It doesn't matter.

When he made the discovery—four dirty-white splash guards severed neatly in half—all chaos broke loose.

There were accusations on his part: "You back the car out of the driveway too fast."

There were threats: "You'll have to pay for new ones."

There were lectures: "Mud flaps are important on a car."

I grew weary. I knew my defense but kept it secret, hoping he would lose interest.

He did not.

"I will tell you my drift." —*Much Ado About Nothing*,
Act 2, Scene 1

I couldn't be certain, but I had my suspicions about what had really happened to the mud flaps.

While I had broken one of the first rules of Perfectiondom— carrying too much weight in the car—my mistake had nothing to do with backing out of our driveway.

It had to do, instead, with my generosity.

"There's small choice in rotten apples." —*The Taming Of The Shrew*,
Act 1, Scene 1

Whenever he mentioned the mud flaps, always at the most inopportune of times and always with a glower on his face, I felt the hair rise on the back of my neck.

I wanted him to think that it was at least possible that he had broken them.

It was not easy convincing him, though, because he hardly ever drove that car.

Surely, I told him, trying to be persuasive, he had bounced his way over at least one set of railroad tracks in the past year.

He looked at me peculiarly and growled.

"No legacy is so rich as honesty." —*All's Well That Ends Well,*
Act 2, Scene 5

The truth, which I finally confessed during a weak moment, went like this:

I had picked up my friend and her two grown children and, along with two of my children, we had each done a complete week's worth of grocery shopping. That meant there were probably some eight-hundred pounds of food and flesh distributed in our car and its trunk.

I pulled onto her driveway, which goes up on a steep incline, and, just as she warned, "Don't you think . . . ." we heard a deep, gnarling scratch come from under the auto.

Surprised, we all enjoyed a good, hearty laugh.

"Remuneration! O! That's the Latin word for three farthings!" —
Love's Labour's Lost,
Act 3, Scene 1

But The Perfectionist, who failed to see the humor in my story, got a coup to savor out of it, after all.

Purchasing four new mud flaps at $4.95 per pair, he managed to save forty dollars in service charges by installing them himself.

He glories still in the telling of it.

I Run Over It (Twice)

How do you feel when you're desperate?

"Phenomenon: a rare, significant fact or event. An exceptional, unusual or abnormal person, thing or occurrence." —*Webster's Ninth New Collegiate Dictionary*

I believe it was a phenomenon. The Perfectionist believes that it was an attempt on my part to ruin not only our vacation but our vehicle, and quite possibly our marriage, as well.

Picture if you can, a southbound, silver hubcap—of unknown origin—on a mission.

It has all the personality and the drive of a seasoned bowling ball. It is determined. It is unwavering. It moves in a straight line as if set in motion by a steady but unseen hand.

It is rolling down the center of an unfamiliar road at great speed, probably well over seventy miles per hour, and it appears to be unstoppable.

And then there's us.

The Perfectionist has done his time driving north. The day is perfect: blue sky, a sparkling sun, a gentle breeze.

Why don't I take a turn driving so he can relax for a while, he suggests.

I am agreeable.

He stops the car. We exchange seats. I depress the gas pedal and he lays back, cocked at an angle between the seat and the door. His eyelids are at half-mast, just covering eyeballs that are looking but not really seeing, and he is at peace.

The car is moving along with a gentle hum. I am enjoying the view.

Suddenly, from out of nowhere there is the hubcap, hugging without mercy the yellow line that divides the highway.

And just as suddenly, The Perfectionist is upright, clutching at a door handle. His eyes are wide, but he refrains from speaking.

I can read his mind, thinking in capitals: DO NOT HIT THE HUBCAP. I am trapped. There is a backseat driver to the right of me, a rogue hubcap to the left.

Oh, dread.

Of course, I do not want to hit the hubcap. My problem is I can't decide which direction it is rolling and where I should go to avoid it.

The hubcap's motion is that of an optical illusion. It appears to be moving in the same direction that we are—and although I am slowing the car, we seem to be gaining on it.

On the other hand, it seems to be coming at us from the opposite direction. I brake and pull to the right as fast as I dare. I don't want to run off the road at this speed. And I don't want to confuse the driver who is tailgating me.

The hubcap makes its way under us and my heart sinks.

I look at The Perfectionist, who appears volcano-like: he is rigid and his nostrils flare to emit smoke with each merciless bang of metal on metal.

There goes the brake line. There goes the gas tank. There goes the muffler. There goes the exhaust system, altogether.

There goes the mystique of marriage.

The Perfectionist Makes a Mistake

Can you juggle?

My mother's Siamese is, as she puts it, "Worse than a kid!" The phone rings, and the cat is instantly at her side, begging for attention.

Mother doesn't realize it, but she should count her blessings. She can toss the animal a cat yummy, without breaking her pace or routine, and immediately all is well.

Life with The Perfectionist is not that easy.

All the tricks in the world will not appease the man when he is on a quest, and I am on the phone.

Last week, I was deep into a telephone conversation with my neighbor Beverly when The Perfectionist came into the kitchen and demanded to know where I had left the car keys.

For him, this was a matter that couldn't wait.

I pointed out that the large white appendage adjoining my ear was a telephone receiver, but he paid me no mind.

He asked me about the keys again, and I grew hostile.

Oh, would that I had stereophonic ears!

Maybe it's me, but I can't listen to two people at the same time and concentrate on what each is saying.

When I got off the phone I was angry and worried. The truth was, I hadn't the foggiest idea where the keys were.

Fortunately, The Perfectionist went outside to collect himself.

Not wanting to admit that I had lost them, I began a panicked search, recounting the steps I had taken before the telephone rang.

Let's see: I had picked up four children, three of them ages six or younger, from swimming; bought them all ice cream cones; driven them home and attempted to get them, their wet bodies, their wet towels, their shoes, their spare clothes and, most importantly, their sticky hands into the house without incident.

The Perfectionist disdains incidents.

I piled the wet clothes in a safe place, tossed out two half-eaten, soggy cones, wiped off eight sets of fingers (five fingers per set), and quickly put a movie into the VCR before one of the children could decide to do it for himself.

The Perfectionist disdains tampering with the VCR.

I retraced my steps about the house with no luck. I felt my pockets a record five times. I shuffled through the kids' belongings. I turned over the couch cushions. I called Beverly to see if the keys somehow made it to her house after I took her children home. (My son decided to vomit, naturally, and I returned them a little bit early.)

I also searched the garbage.

Finally, I had to admit to The Perfectionist that I simply could not find the keys.

The Perfectionist loves it when I am in this kind of predicament. He thinks I am disorganized.

He also loves an opportunity to lecture. (I have often suggested that he give up his profession and join the lecture circuit.)

"If you'd hung them up on the hook where they belong, this wouldn't have happened," he intoned.

Imagine my euphoria when the truth finally presented itself.

Reviewing the events that had led up to the keys' disappearance, I tried to make The Perfectionist understand the confusion that comes with little children when, suddenly, I remembered that I had asked him to retrieve something from the car's trunk.

You guessed it! The keys were in his pocket.

Beverly Hits a High Note

What do you do at the poor house?

Mothers,
Do you sing at night
Of the little things that made your day?
Or do you store them, between quilts
In a hope chest
And pray that the best
Is yet to come?

Two questions arose, after much turmoil, at this week's garage sale: Is it possible to nickel-and-dime one's way to a fortune? And, is it worth it?

Consider the case of poor Beverly. She volunteered her garage for the neighborhood sale, but she left me in charge of two signs, and I put them out forty-five minutes early.

It was an innocent move on my part. I wanted them out before my daughter's school bus arrived. Weren't most shoppers busy getting their own children off to school? I reasoned.

No, they were not. They were barreling their ways down the road that leads to Beverly's house.

Beverly, who severely sprained her wrist recently, has three children under the age of five. Suffice it to say she was harried on the morning in question. The children all needed feeding, dressing and brushing. In addition, the oldest needed his school bag—and an item he had confiscated, unbeknownst to his mother, from the garage sale display.

For some reason, he felt compelled to debate with her, at the last minute, whether or not he should take said item to show-and-tell.

Beverly, exasperated, relented and, with scarcely a moment to spare, looked up to see the garbage truck arriving, like the garage-salers, much too early.

Ah! The vision she made! Standing in her kitchen expertly spinning a huge garbage bag closed. Launching herself from the hallway landing. Jostling the bag around garage sale items and patrons with the nerve of a race car driver. Hurrying it to the curb with her long hair flying.

Beverly beat the truck with just enough time to wonder: Oh! Could she beat the kindergarten bus as well?

There was time, she decided, if she hurried. In a flash, Beverly and her son sprinted behind their house, bound for the corner a block away. At last sighting, the child was laughing. And Beverly was pumping her arms.

All morning long, strangers trekked in and out of Beverly's house—where she had corralled four busy toddlers—for a look at the large desk she was selling.

Was it a roll top? they asked her one-by-one.

No, but it had belonged to two millionaires before she and her husband refinished it, she told them.

The reference was one of only a few Beverly made about her husband during the sale. He would not participate in or go to garage sales, she said emphatically.

But he was not above interrupting them to ask favors.

The phone rang. I saw Beverly dart from the garage to the kitchen, grab the phone, place its receiver on the counter, hurry into the dining room, strike a chord on the piano and return to the phone.

She hummed a long, beautiful B-flat into its mouthpiece.

"Mark needed a note," was her simple explanation to those of us who stood wondering in her garage.

Abruptly, Beverly realized it was time for the kindergarten bus to return home. Where had the morning gone?

She stepped out of the garage, flapped her arms at her sides, birdlike, and screamed.

It was only after she returned from the bus stop with her son, made six lunch sandwiches, put her baby in a box for safe-keeping and sat down that Beverly came to a realization.

While no one had taken the desk, somebody, thank heaven, had finally purchased one of her two toilet training potties.

As Erma Bombeck would have said: "What does it profiteth a woman?"

Mrs. X Hears a Voice

What does "get real" mean?

As she grew older, Mrs. X found it harder and harder to sleep at night.

It seemed to her, when she lay frustrated and staring into the darkness during the wee hours, like every noise within a ten-mile radius of her bed caught the attention of her ears.

She heard the furnace groan beneath its own weight. She heard the refrigerator click on. She heard her neighbor come home from the late shift.

She heard her dog scratch itself and yawn in its cage, four rooms over.

Mrs. X knew (oh, she was jealous all right) that the dog would get its itch, curl into a ball and go back to sleep without any trouble.

"Dratted dog," she said, shifting onto her right side and wishing for just one good night's sleep.

Mrs. X lifted her head slightly from her pillow then adjusted it down so that her right ear flap was tucked under its adjoining ear.

Plugged.

Then she stared ahead, into the void, pulled her blanket up close to her chin and raised her left hand to cover her other ear.

It worked, and for a while she lay in the darkness with her elbow aimed at the ceiling.

Mrs. X couldn't hear anything. And she couldn't get comfortable in that position either. Unwelcome thoughts that provoked the problem came to Mrs. X during those wakeful nights.

She lay in her bed and wondered when the ability to go into a quick and peaceful sleep had actually left her.

Used to be she could fall under the covers, position her pillow and drift easily into a dream that would carry her through the night.

In fact, it used to be when she was a child, that she could fall out of the bed completely, crawl back in, and be asleep in a matter of seconds.

Sleep is wasted on the young, she thought.

Lying there, Mrs. X figured her troubles began when she had children of her own. She'd trained herself to hear their coughs and faint cries during the night and had added children to her family, one by one, until some fifteen years had passed.

Mrs. X knew her bladder was part of her problem too.

Somewhere along the line, it had failed her.

Mrs. X glanced at the clock across the room. It said 3:53 a.m.

She threw back the covers and rose from her bed onto her stiff legs. Mrs. X had been down the hallway in the dark so many times that she could now make her way without feeling along the walls.

She came to the bathroom—it was pitch black—pushed on its door and groped for the light switch.

"I'm in here," she heard the deep, disgusted voice of her husband say in measured tones.

Mrs. X yanked her hand back to her side and turned to retrace her steps.

This must have been what it was like for Dorothy encountering the great and powerful Oz, she thought.

A foreboding voice. The dark. A dog.

Mrs. X turned back to her bed. She knew that, unlike Dorothy, she would probably never get her wish.

Lavatoriphobia

Did you know that skunk smells are the strongest in the world?

I have the following fantasy: The Perfectionist and I arrive at a restaurant, any restaurant, for a leisurely meal.

The hostess, her face aglow with a smile, greets us warmly as we move in from the door.

"Good evening," she says, "a table for two?"

We nod our heads affirmatively, our eyes adjusting to the dim lights, and the hostess continues, "Bathroom or no bathroom?"

I glance at The Perfectionist with a satisfied look. I have been waiting all of my adult life for this moment.

"No bathroom," I reply.

Unruffled, the hostess says, "Please follow me," and calmly escorts us to a cozy little booth in a corner of the dining room set way apart from the restaurant's, ahem, facilities. We proceed to dine in absolute bliss.

While I dislike eating my meals under a shroud of smoke produced by other diners, and therefore appreciate being allowed a seat in a nonsmoking section in a restaurant, I find it even more disagreeable to be seated at a table near a toilet, especially when I want to relax.

Call it what you will. A bugaboo, a fixation, a pet peeve. (Lavatoriphobia seems a good word.) But it honestly seems to me that in one lifetime, I have been ushered to every bathroom-adjacent table in every restaurant I've eaten in between New York City and Los Angeles, from Mackinaw City to Miami.

For me, the ultimate frustration comes in those eateries that are all but vacant when I arrive.

The following scenario happens too often: A hostess (you've seen them all do it) surveys the dining room with her eyes as if seeking out the most intimate booth.

Finding one that appeals to her, she takes a few misleading steps toward it then summons me by dangling a wrist above her head and flicking two fingers through the air.

As I follow, the hostess suddenly changes her course, making an unexpected detour in the direction of the lavatory with me in disgusted pursuit, mumbling, "It figures."

It seems a plot and not a coincidence.

This aversion of mine has little to do with aesthetics (porcelain or otherwise) or the sounds of repeated flushes drowning out fascinating conversation.

Instead, it has a lot to do with people forming parade lines past my chair when I am trying to eat.

I believe this phobia is a hereditary, sex-linked, female-dominant trait (my mother is this way) that first manifests itself after a woman becomes a mother.

Lavatoriphobia begins when an infant graduates to the stage of toddler and said toddler develops the habit of saying, "Mommy, I have to go to the bathroom," during dinner.

Mommy must then abandon her meat loaf to assist the toddler.

The phobia becomes exacerbated (this is a medical term that loosely translates into "full-blown worse") when the toddler, joined by his/her siblings, realizes his/her independence and begins jumping up from the table at random to go to the toilet, answer the door, fetch the ketchup and, when he/she becomes a teenager, to answer the telephone, which rings precisely at fork lift-off time.

Fathers, quite obviously, do not come down with Lavatoriphobia.

They can sympathize, however, because they oftentimes fall victim to Plugged-privyitis, a lesser known though potentially more odious condition.

Accompanying a stopped-up toilet, its symptoms include plunger-induced sore biceps and an overwhelming desire not to dine out.

The male, bless his anatomy, would rather take a long fishing trip near a woods.

Rockin' Without The Perfectionist

Why is it I have that song stuck in my head?

"I am," I told The Perfectionist last week, "going to go and wallow in nostalgia."

Just thinking about the possibilities filled me with pleasure. I smiled and offered him a hug.

"You are," he corrected me with a matter-of-fact tone, "going to go and wallow in twenty-five percent of nostalgia."

Technically, he was right, but I hugged him anyway. And then I set off happily, sixty-five dollars in hand, to purchase two tickets to see Paul McCartney in concert.

Before I left, I asked The Perfectionist if he would like to accompany me to the show. It might be his only chance to see this century's greatest living musician, a former Beatle! I told him.

Wouldn't he, I asked, have gone to see Mozart?

The Perfectionist shrugged and declined my invitation, saying that he would have gone to see Elvis. (I knew better than to contest his decision. How many times have we debated who was greater and more popular: Elvis or the Beatles? There are no winners in these arguments.)

So I called my daughter, off at college, and invited her instead.

"Who? Hey, that would be cool," she said calmly.

She sounded like she was in the middle of a swallow. I could envision her weighing the pros and cons of attending this concert with her middle-aged mother.

Finally, she asked me, "You're not going to throw your underwear on stage, are you?"

I remember vividly the morning in 1966 when my mother (bless her rock-n-roll loving, understanding soul) called my sister and me down from our bedrooms to announce that she had family tickets to a Beatles concert in Detroit.

I was fifteen years old, my sister was thirteen, and the Beatles were at the height of their fame. Together, in that instant, my sister and I became—for the only time in our lives—a single, gyrating mass of screaming flesh.

Oh, euphoria!

"I still have my ticket stub from that concert," I told The Perfectionist as I moved toward the door.

It is green and it says, "Sec. 19, Row A, Seat 5, Olympia Stadium. Sat. Mat. 2:00 p.m. Aug. 13, 1966." It also says, "balcony $4.50."

"Just think," I said to The Perfectionist, "it cost my parents $4.50 per ticket to take us to see the Beatles."

The Perfectionist, standing over his coffee cup, pulled a pen out of his shirt pocket and did some quick figuring.

"Well, this time," he said, "you're going to see one of them at seven times the price."

Of course, he was right. But it is hard to put a price tag on nostalgia. (Incidentally noted: There was a $4.50 service charge for each $32.50 McCartney ticket.)

My Goose Gets Cooked

How do you avoid temptation?

Word has it that there are monks and priests in some other cultures who, with years of very intensive training and practical experience, can levitate their prone bodies into the air. Will them upwards, if you will.

In some circles, this great feat is considered to be a mystery.

At our house, I have come to realize, levitation should be the expected result of any of a number of good ideas.

For example, recently my son approached me with a pair of old, hole-ridden blue jeans that were about six inches too short for him, and he pointed out the fact that they had become virtually useless. He then asked me what should be done with them.

"We might as well burn them," I suggested, assuming no one else could possibly want them in that condition. My son reacted favorably, throwing them, kid-style, into a heap in his bedroom for a later date with destiny.

I completely forgot about the pants until one evening—just as The Perfectionist arrived home after a long day.

He entered the kitchen, plopped his briefcase on the cupboard, sparked a flame under the tea kettle and listened, sort of with one half-hearing ear, while our son came into the room carrying his pants across one arm.

"I thought you were going to burn these," our son said, addressing me with confusion and a scowl.

Pfftt!

Just like that, in one smooth movement, The Perfectionist arose into the air. Up he went where he could have counted the dust particles on the top of my refrigerator, if he really wanted to.

Alas, he didn't really want to.

He came down from above wearing a Perfectionistic glower and he bellowed,

"Don't tell her that!"

The very apples in my fruit bin rattled in response.

I tend to forget that The Perfectionist has problems with my burning things. He has frightening memories of the time I singed our house cat in our early-model gas oven; and recalls with a shudder the time he came home from work to find our backyard fully ablaze and me beating it with a broom.

I have figured out how to get around his fears, though. Now I just don't tell him when I plan to burn something.

Take this case in point:

For years I had been vacuuming around an old, mildewed and disgusting, yellowed pillow that once belonged to The Perfectionist's mother. He was saving it for that nebulous "someday when we might be able to use it" that men so highly favor.

Finally, I just couldn't stand it anymore.

Leaving it in its equally odious pillowcase, I gleefully threw it into the fireplace one afternoon when I was alone. I then set it—oh, how shall I call it?

Ablaze?

No, it wouldn't burn.

Alight?

No, it wouldn't catch.

I set it asmoulder is what I did. And this in February—in Michigan.

Little-by-little the pillowcase melted away, revealing as it did so, through a deep, black shroud of smoke that completely filled our family room, at least four gooses' worth of plucked feathers.

Am I a baby-booming-foam-rubber lover or what?

Born too late in the era to be knowledgeable, it never occurred to me that there might be feathers in that pillow. And I don't know about new ones, but fifty-year-old goose feathers do not burn.

Do not panic, I told myself, flapping just a little, myself, before jabbing at the mess with a fireplace poker and forcing a thick plume of soot into the air.

I blew on the feathers some, hoping to inspire a more generous flame and I checked my watch.

As you can probably imagine, time had flown where no goose had flown before.

The Perfectionist levitated his way into the family room just as I was opening the doorwall to let in a little five-degree, February air.

"Ah, the sweet smells of Nature," I said, by way of greeting. I was on tiptoes, smiling my way through the incredible smell as I attempted to rise above the smoke.

So much for my burning desires.

The Hock-A-Loogie Chorus

Have you ever tried to hold your breath and talk at once?

I am not really sure of the correct terminology or spelling. I don't know if it's "Hark! A lewgie!" or "Huck, a lougie?" or "Hock-a-loogie."

What I do know is that somehow I got implicated in a most foul scheme. It began when I attempted to do a good deed.

I reasoned: What is a mother if not a good role model? What are sports without good sportsmanship?

Sure, I said, I would be willing to transport another boy to and from karate class with my son. No problem.

That was my first mistake.

On only our second trip, the boy in question, age ten, having assessed me as a pushover and my child as a pigeon, taught my son (barely age seven at the time, and a complete innocent) how to make armpit/belching noises while I dodged traffic and turned gray.

On the return trip, he brought up the subject of loogies—my preferred spelling—and my son was enthralled.

Now, part of my problem may be that I am used to raising daughters. They are a different breed entirely.

Whenever I drove them with their friends to some childhood activity, they sang, or listened to the radio, or at their absolute worst, giggled.

I never considered that two boys in a back seat would be any different.

"What's a loogie? What's a loogie?" my son begged to know.

I shushed the sneering ten-year-old until I couldn't take the sound of my son's voice anymore.

"Okay, go ahead and tell him," I said, finally, somewhat curious to hear the boy's explanation myself.

Granting a ten-year-old that kind of permission was my second mistake.

He seized the moment and commenced a graphic demonstration, forcing his nostrils together and summoning a snorting noise that seemed to go on forever.

Catching his breath and saying, "First you sniff . . . ," he then continued with what can only be described as a reverse snort—one that began in his nether regions and worked its way up to his throat, violently—bringing with it a variety of body fluids.

He pinched his lips together and smiled at his achievement.

"Then you mix . . . ," he went on, talking around his tongue and the wad it was controlling.

I could contain myself no longer. I took my eyes off traffic and turned to tell him to please not spit out my car window.

I never got the chance.

Before I could speak, my little innocent, who had been observing intently, offered up the following while gazing solemnly at his friend, "Hey! My mom does that!"

Baked to Perfection

Why can't you keep the bone after you eat the chicken?

I have endured a colorful and varied tenure as a cook.

I have unwittingly scorched the family cat in the oven, automatically self-cleaned (behind a locked oven door) a $7 roast, and have made, unintentionally, a set of zucchini-flavored doorstops.

Of the three, it was the doorstops, seasoned with cinnamon, that filled our house with the most delicious and tempting aroma.

As you can imagine, the cat was by far the most offensive-smelling item that I have baked. And the most allergy-producing.

That is until this week when I set about the task of baking four karate boards.

I can now say with all sincerity that, as a cook, I have done it all.

There is some discussion among karate mothers about the proper technique for cooking boards.

Some mothers microwave theirs before putting them in the oven, getting a jump on the drying process, as it were.

Some heat theirs for only a couple of hours, tempting fate with a higher temperature than is recommended—and therefore risking burning. And others bake theirs not once but twice, to ensure that the boards are sufficiently primed for breaking by hand or foot.

Two weeks ago today, my son's karate instructor told me, unexpectedly, that it was time, at long last, for us to buy boards.

Selecting a board was, to my surprise, somewhat harder than selecting a roast—or a cat, for that matter.

I was told to: Examine the available boards visually and check for knot holes. Pick up each board with my hands and buy the one that felt like it weighed the least. Get pine.

I had a lot of fun thinking about the possibilities before I made my purchase.

To begin with, my son only weighs forty-five pounds—and that is on a good day when he has had three well-balanced meals, a morning and afternoon snack, and his hair is still wet from the shower.

I can't picture him breaking any board with those ruler-thin arms of his. But I spent a little time, anyway, imagining what it would be like for him if I bought, say, oak or redwood.

It was a cruel thought, wasn't it?

There are three types of businesses that I do not enjoy patronizing. They are: automobile repair stations, heating and cooling shops, and lumberyards.

I do not enjoy them because I do not enjoy shopping in male-dominated arenas. Thus, self-consciously, I slinked into the local lumberyard behind a few men who were wearing their work clothes and mid-day whiskers, and I awaited my turn at the cash register.

When I said, in the deepest voice I could muster, "I need to buy a karate board," all the men in the shop turned to stare.

The clerk asked me how many feet of board I wanted, and I had to do math in my head, which doubled my agony.

Then we went out to the yard to make a selection.

What do I know from boards?

I picked up several, balanced them in my hands, eyed them front and back, and took the first one handed to me.

That night, The Perfectionist sawed them into eight-inch lengths, and the next day I popped them into the oven in preparation for a tournament.

As they cooked, I would occasionally slip on a pot holder mitten, pull the tray of boards out, rearrange them so they cooked evenly, and check for burned spots.

Then I would shove them back into the oven and sneeze as the aroma of pine filled my kitchen.

I sneezed for two days.

Mrs. X Gets the Creeps

How many arms do you wish we had?

Mrs. X gathered about her what she thought seemed like the necessary tools: rubber physician's gloves, a flashlight, tweezers, a magnifying glass, and the camp counselor's letter, which, after she had read it, made her itch all over.

She arranged the items on the bathroom counter in a semicircle, prayed quickly for a good hunt, and called to her little daughter.

The child arrived with her ponytail bouncing and a smile on her face. Only five years old, she seemed to Mrs. X so innocent. Still fresh and new.

Mrs. X did not want to frighten her daughter with thoughts of the awful-awful, so with little explanation she gave the girl a hug and then slowly pulled the rubber band from her hair.

"Let me have a look," was all she said, tilting the child's face toward the floor.

"When we're done here, I'll show you how to inflate these gloves into rooster balloons," she added, and she snapped them onto her hands.

Mrs. X felt the weight of the girl's thick, shimmering hair slide across the gloves. She let it fall slowly, separating the strands gently as if the hair were no more than a handful of wispy cotton. Then she looked toward the counter so she could reread the letter.

"Please be informed," it began, "that cases of head lice have been reported at the camp . . . ."

"What a life," Mrs. X mumbled.

Cringing, Mrs. X picked up the flashlight and clutched at the girl's hair. Unable to see clearly, she set the flashlight down and picked up the magnifying glass. She clutched the hair again, but there wasn't enough light for her to see.

Mrs. X was at a loss, and she fumbled. She mumbled under her breath that she wished she had more hands.

Moving with her daughter to a picture window, where the afternoon's sunlight could add its assistance, Mrs. X raked her fingers through the girl's hair, and she took a long, hard look.

Her worst fears were confirmed.

She shuddered and made a dash for the phone. Before long, she heard the friendly voice of an office clerk.

"Yes, the doctor will speak with you if you could just hold for a moment."

Mrs. X didn't know very many pediatricians who would come to the phone during office hours. That was one thing she especially liked about this man.

She waited, imagining the coming siege: A frenzy of vacuuming, washing, dusting.

She would have to shampoo and then attack all four children with a fine-toothed comb. With any luck they wouldn't need to have their heads shaved.

In addition, she figured, she would probably have to give the cat a bath.

Oh, dread.

Mrs. X heard the doctor come on the line.

"I think my daughter has contracted head lice," she told him, and she was filled with embarrassment. "Could I bring her in for you to check and make sure?"

Mrs. X pictured the doctor with his impish eyes, his thatch of thick, curly hair and his full beard, talking to her from a hallway phone.

"No. No," he said for the first time in her experience, and Mrs. X knew that he was begging on behalf of his beard.

That's when it occurred to her that she was glad she had been born female.

The Find

How would you like it if you had gum stuck to your chin?

I read in a newspaper a couple of weeks ago that an archeologist recently found a piece of prehistoric gum while excavating.

This was considered to be a big find, historically and scientifically speaking, since the gum still contained the teeth marks of the cave teenager who had chewed it.

In addition, the professionals who study these things were able to determine some of the gum's contents.

Oh, rounds of great jubilation!

Of course, what they don't know is what the teen was doing when he disposed of the gum.

Probably driving his mother nuts.

Picture it: A Friday night. He has completed his chores, badgered his siblings for a while and groomed himself for the upcoming weekend happening. He has an important date—a first date—and he is anxious.

Pacing as he awaits the passage of time, the teenager dips into his pocket and retrieves a wad of Dino-Mo-Blo. He pushes it over his lips and between his teeth, disfiguring his cheek while he works it down to a manageable size.

He sighs, relaxing as his jaws take the edge off his jitters, shrugs his hands into his pockets and leans against the cave wall. He is not thinking when he cracks it loudly once, then twice, within earshot of his weary mother.

She loses her patience quickly.

"Why don't you get rid of that awful mouthful?" she asks. "Your date won't find it attractive, and neither do I."

Hearing his friends round the curve to his dwelling, he takes his mother's advice just this once and pulls the gum, sticky, from his mouth to chuck it with forefinger and thumb into history.

Thousands of years later, maybe even millions, a group of enthusiastic explorers find it and consider themselves lucky.

Nobody bothers to ask how all this affected the teen's poor mother. I mean, maybe it got lodged in her daughter's hair, and she had to spend her Friday night cutting it out against the protestations of a crying child.

Or maybe, during all those centuries, it stuck to her decomposing sofa, leaving a nasty, irremovable spot.

My sympathies lay with the mother, as you can tell.

Last week, I was cleaning my kitchen—the one I recently painted and redecorated. I wiped a little here and rearranged a little there, making it look as attractive as possible.

Finally, I decided to shove over my microwave and wipe away the accumulating dust. I mustered all my strength and gave a big push against its weight.

You guessed it!

There, behind the microwave, was a piece of hard, green, tooth-marked gum, miles away from the garbage bag. I chipped it off the counter, threw it away and brought the matter up over dinner.

"Does anybody know how the wad of gum got behind the microwave?" I asked.

Those present looked among themselves. Of course, no one would admit guilt.

By the time I learn who's responsible, I'll probably be a fossil myself.

The Kiss

What is a shock?

At seventy, she could have been anybody's grandmother.

Her breasts, heavy with age, rested sluggishly atop a belt that held her housedress snugly about her waist while two nylon-encased legs, choking under the pressure of elastic garters, peeked out from beneath its hem.

Decades spent standing over stoves and mops and pails, coupled with a childhood case of rheumatic fever, had put a large dowager's hump square in the middle of her back.

Thick, grease-caked glasses brought the world within viewing distance of her cloudy brown eyes.

And her teeth?

Like the beauty of her youth, they were long since forgotten.

The one existing picture of her as a little girl always elicited a gasp of surprise from anyone viewing it for the first time.

"That's her?" people would ask.

It was hard to believe.

The little girl in the picture was truly beautiful. Her lustrous black hair cascaded down her shoulders, topped by an enormous gingham bow. Her large eyes hinted at a joyous childhood. And a touch of a smile crossed her lips as she reached for the one toy she owned: her beloved doll.

Nowadays, when she wasn't complaining about something, or asking someone to repeat himself for the zillionth time, or predicting doom for somebody, she would affectionately reminisce about those happy girlhood days.

They offered a stark contrast to her lonely, old-age existence.

It was easy to wonder about the many experiences, like not being able to marry the man she loved, that made her, well, so testy with age.

On this day, she struggled to force open the door of the car, wondering aloud how she was going to walk all the way from the parking lot to the amphitheater.

"I'll never make it," she said to her son, huffing dramatically as she took her first steps.

"Yes, you will," he replied, grasping her elbow and leading her forward, determined that, against all odds, she was going to have a good time. Theirs was a ponderous, long walk.

Arriving finally, he eased her into a lawn chair on the hill and attempted to cheer her with talk of the upcoming outdoor concert. Her first.

It wasn't easy.

Behind them, pouring himself yet another glass of wine, sat a dark, good-looking, middle-aged man who was fairly exuding cheerfulness.

He struck up a conversation laden with friendly small talk while offering them samples of the cheeses and fruits he had brought to the concert on a platter.

He seemed an unlikely Prince Charming.

Throughout the evening, this stranger continued to share his food, wine and friendship, making sure that he included "Grandma" (as he called her), who was complaining as usual.

From the glint in his eyes, it appeared clear to others that this man recognized an old woman's contrariness when he saw it. And it was also clear that he intended to do something about it.

As the music wound down and the theatergoers began to pack up their belongings, Prince Charming completed the evening as only he could have.

He bent down over "Grandma" and, puckering, planted a large, juicy kiss full on her thin, shrunken lips.

What a moment!

Stunned, then pleased, "Grandma" came back to life.

Mrs. Lookadoo

Why do we have two hands?

The birds have found Mrs. Lookadoo's bird feeder.

They come to it frequently now—cardinals, sparrows and other varieties that I cannot yet identify—and they eat while I wash my dishes.

The feeder is perched on a long pole planted deep in the earth outside my kitchen window, and it is as safe as I can make it in this age.

Every now and then I offer up a quick prayer that no one will steal it. Such things have been known to happen in our neighborhood.

I felt a twinge of guilt when I plucked the feeder from Mrs. Lookadoo's yard.

It had stood for at least twenty years off a sitting room at her large and aging home. It overlooked a pond, a stream and an expanse of peaceful woodsy property.

I moved it on a cold day when there was no sun.

I had only been to Mrs. Lookadoo's house on one previous occasion, years ago, when I went to interview her for an article I was writing.

I sought her out because she was old enough to remember the old lady I was researching.

Mrs. Lookadoo welcomed me into her home with a glass of lemonade. It was her pleasure to recall for me the subject of my story.

Long dead, the old lady had been a gifted photographer, artist and seamstress, Mrs. Lookadoo said.

As so often happens during interviews, the formalities quickly went by the wayside, and the question-and-answer period fell easily into pleasant conversation.

I listened while Mrs. Lookadoo drifted into stories about her own life. She loved rabbits.

Quite unexpectedly, Mrs. Lookadoo went upstairs to a bedroom.

The seamstress of my story had, at one time, created for Mrs. Lookadoo a little rabbit from a white kid glove, she told me as she ascended the stairs. Its two ears were fashioned from fingers.

Mrs. Lookadoo was certain that she could find the rabbit for me, and I heard her rummaging. After a spell, she began calling to me: Could I try to open a drawer?

I followed her voice to the bedroom, where she gave me a ruler to push about inside a cocked, jammed drawer that had been closed for years. I felt uncomfortable prodding her dresser, but I was successful.

The kid glove rabbit was there, as charmed as the *Velveteen Rabbit*, and I fell in love with it just as I did Mrs. Lookadoo.

I intended after that to visit her again.

So it was on a blustery day, several years later, lured by signs, that I made my way into Mrs. Lookadoo's home with an assortment of strangers.

I hate estate sales. At them, the things that people have cherished most in their lives—their memories—go to the highest bidders.

I tried, but I could not find the little glove rabbit. The people organizing the sale supposed that her daughter had taken it.

Finally, determined that I would buy something to remember her by, I chose the bird feeder.

I hope that in some small way the beauty of her kind and gentle soul flourishes in my yard.

I Am Launched

Have you ever been on a roller coaster?

Wasn't it enough of a challenge that after a long and trying week (during which I worked, wifed and parented) I had settled down to grapple with Capt. Kirk and the "Guardian of Forever?"

Picture me, late on that particular Friday night, trying to concentrate on space languages, descriptions of aliens, strange thought patterns, and complex intergalactic problems while my eyelids grew heavy.

Frankly, I was cranky—though apparently somebody "out there" didn't care. For along came my young son, guided perhaps by my vulnerability.

He chose that particular night—the one where I had just eased myself into The Perfectionist's brand new La-Z-Boy chair, pumped up my feet, leaned back into folds of welcoming cushions, and turned a page of a book—to approach me and ask every parent's all-time favorite question:

"What is sex?"

I put the Star Trek book in my lap and drove my head so deep into the back of the chair that I could hear the graying hairs on my scalp grating between corduroy and flesh.

I stretched out full-length and stared blankly at the ceiling, hoping that somewhere in that great white expanse I might find the answer. Or better yet, some wiser-than-me someone to deliver it.

Where was Mr. Spock when I needed him?

It seems to me that children have an uncanny sixth sense that they turn to whenever they have questions like that and: a) the timing is bad, b) there is no father handy, or c) a mother has let her guard down.

(The Perfectionist, of course, was in bed, snoring happily, oblivious to this ages-old question and all of its implications. You can bet that what was about to transpire would never have happened to him.)

Sensing my discomfort at his question, the boy worked his way closer to the chair, ever the more intrigued.

He is a long boy, slim and pliable as a snake.

He stood over the out-stretched me and peered down into my face, straight into my glossed-over eyes like he was peering into a pool of murky water. Then, smoothly, he swung a leg up near the side of my head.

Following the leg came a hip and then a shoulder and soon he was beside me in his entirety, waiting expectantly for an answer that just wasn't going to come.

I decided to stall for time when suddenly I felt the chair begin to shift.

I was about to boldly go where no one in our family had gone before.

In one smooth motion, under the additional weight of my son, the La-Z-Boy became a catapult, and I became, a what? A mind-boggled human projectile on a mission for answers?

No, I was a dud is what I was.

I landed, wham! on the top of my head, wedged firmly between the over-turned chair, the wall, the piano, and a table while, somehow, to his credit, my son managed to evacuate.

"Go get your father," I said, as he ran around in a panic.

He fled to the bedroom and returned to tell me that The Perfectionist had raised his head off his pillow, rolled over, and gone back to sleep.

"You must go get your father. I can't get out," I emphasized, trying to be serious, though I was laughing to the point where tears were traveling down my face. (Actually, since I was upside-down they were traveling up my face.)

Anyway, the boy disappeared again and a few minutes later The Perfectionist emerged from the bedroom. His thinning hair was askew. His jowls were set. His nostrils pulsed.

With what looked like a Herculean effort from my perspective, he pushed the footrest of the La-Z-Boy with two hands and slammed me and the chair into an upright position. The speed and accuracy of his effort would have amazed even mission control!

And he never said a word.

Of course, you realize that by not speaking, The Perfectionist managed, like the elusive Mr. Spock, to dodge that ages-old question:

"What is sex?"

Miscarriage

Is zero an even number?

It is a Friday afternoon, and I am sitting in my quiet computer room, alone. Beside me, the window of our old house lets in a little October sunlight. That light brings with it the colors of changing leaves—the colors of time marching—and as it does so, it throws various shades of Nature's reds upon me.

They are shades that, for some reason, bring back memories on days like this.

I can hear humming coming from the printer atop my desk, and the telephone waits patiently—as if it expects that sometime soon it will have a message to relay. If the telephone rings, I know that there will be life on the other end of it when I answer.

The people who share my days with me have gone their own ways for a while. Papers and toys and half-empty glasses lie where they abandoned them. They are an evidence of sorts. Proof that somebody was here, and proof that somebody expects to be back.

I can see nothing of the drivers who slow their cars as they drive past our house and stop for the stop sign. And I can see nothing of the pedestrians who walk their dogs up and down our street, or the birds that fleck nearby tree limbs, or the sky that stands watch over them, come what may.

I know, of course, that while I cannot see them, they are nevertheless real.

I am in a pensive mood. There is a certain thought nudging at me. It wants expression.

I know before I begin typing that if I am to shape that thought I shall have to go deep within myself. The words that will give the thought life reside somewhere in my soul. I want them to make their way to the page, and so I begin.

Sitting here, looking at my computer screen and thinking, I watch the tiny, black cursor blink on and off against a gray background, in an even rhythm before me.

On, off. On, off.

It reminds me of a heartbeat I once watched symbolized on a similar monitor.

The heartbeat came from within me, but it was not mine. It was that of a five-week-old fetus, represented by a tiny shining light on an ultrasound screen.

I watched it beat, and I was filled with excitement and hope. On, off. On, off. It was a comfort to know that there was life making that cursor pulse.

Three months later that life was gone.

What amazes me now, even after all these years—and still could make me cry—is the realization that while that life was once thriving inside of mine, it left unexpectedly one day—without a struggle, or a shout, or even a good-bye to its mother—and I did not know the difference.

Shouldn't I have felt that life leaving my body? Shouldn't I have sensed it going, somehow?

I have wondered since, on days like this when I allow my mind its freedom, what I was doing at the very moment that life passed from mine.

Perhaps I was preparing a meal. Perhaps I was driving. Perhaps I was embracing one of my other children.

Maybe that life left during an argument. Or maybe during a prayer.

I have experienced someone else's life inside of my own on four other occasions. I have felt hiccups in the night that weren't mine but that nevertheless kept me awake. And I have felt great, enthusiastic kicks and stretches, some of which prevented me from bending and sitting.

To tell the story of death in the womb—the story of a miscarriage—is to tell of a very private, lonely, painful and misunderstood experience. And yet it is an experience that has affected women too numerous to count.

These women are linked by the truth that even an unseen life is real.

The Imaginary Hug

To my angel friend:

I was embarrassed by my tears of the other day. After all, I came to comfort you as you face the death of your beloved sister. I did not expect to hear the words, "It's okay to cry" coming from your lips.

Instead, I expected to say them to you.

I can only imagine the depth of your grief. How you long to make her well again, if that were only possible. How you wish to take away her physical suffering and make easier that which she must yet face.

I do not need to call upon my powers of imagination to know of your love and faith. I felt them embracing me as we sat talking in your peaceful family room. They went back and forth between us on a flow of gentle, warm words. Back and forth in the unanswerable questions. Back and forth in the hope.

I know that my son felt that love and faith too. And that, in part, is why I am writing you this letter. Because I wept at the time, I could not speak of the profound experience I knew us to be sharing. Even now, tears well up as I search for the right way to say thank you.

Do you know that in that brief hour's conversation, you taught him—showed him—more about compassion, human ties and the love of God than I could in a thousand maternal lectures?

Do you remember how you spoke in a very soft voice with your fingertips moving in the air before you? About how you went to nurse your sister and help her with her most intimate needs?

By explaining your love for her—and hers for you—you elevated those personal acts to ones that seemed almost sacred. I watched as my son sat erect, silent, listening, unafraid.

Do you remember how you spoke of infant love? How you quoted a book that described an old man's last days, and how that old man said a dying person needs love like a baby? How a baby can never get enough?

Do you remember how you spoke then of your adored infant grandson? How you swooped your arms into a great, generous, imaginary hug and said, "Babies are so wonderful"?

I watched as my son leaned forward just a fraction, to be a part of that hug.

Do you remember how you spoke of your mother? Of how you have missed her all these years—and yet know she is waiting for your sister? Do you remember how you said that mothers are so important?

After we left your house, my son said he was filled with an awesome and consuming love for me that was getting on his nerves. And he wondered when the feeling would let up.

I am not worried.

Do you remember how you bowed your head and said, "I took her the Eucharist."? How you slowly passed one hand just over the curved palm of the other and then, looking into my curious son's eyes, explained to him about the body of Christ?

Do you remember how you said that sometimes your faith in God wanes? And how that waning bothers your conscience?

When I first began calling you an angel, the nickname came as a lark. It began, if you will recall, with that case of mistaken identity in your church, and the stranger who screamed when you quietly entered the sanctuary because she had been reading about angels.

More and more I have come to believe that you are an angel, indeed.

Thank you for showing my son that we must act on our love. That we must care for one another, even when it means overcoming our queasiness about the sick and their failing bodies.

Thank you for showing my son that the dying are as important as babies and mothers and hope. Thank you for showing my son that in our humanity we can doubt God one moment, and then share his love in a conversation—or in a wafer scooped into our hands. Thank you for showing my son the beauty of friendship.

Somehow, in that hour, all that is mysterious and wonderful about heaven and earth—and the beings that populate those two places—made themselves manifest. A woman fell ill. A sister loved. A friend cried. A mother watched. A grandmother rejoiced. An angel spoke. God entered in.

And a little boy listened.

Freedom

What is the meaning of life?

There are places in the world where women do not go naked. Where they do not let their forms go free, nor their spirits fly.

By tradition, they are the places of men. Sparse *dojos* set aside long ago for the teaching of the martial arts. Places layered in rules and steeped in the ancient formalities of the Orient.

They are places where the smells of men's skin and sweat vie with those of wood or metal, and sometimes blood, for a place in the air. Where touching is an act that comes from the will, not from the heart. Where whispers and prayers are a rarity. And kisses are an unknown thing.

It was in just such a place that Jennifer chose to show her breasts. To release them from bondage the way all women wish they could. If only they were brave enough. Or simple enough, like Jennifer.

It was in just such a place that Jennifer chose to convert her breasts into the misplaced wings they were meant to be.

Jennifer's breasts came to her at the appropriate time in her life— during the early teenage years. They came to her despite the fact that her mind lagged years behind them and her body had the carriage and the awkward shape of a dwarf child's. Her breasts went before her, like mastheads before a storm, and they carried enough weight so that they sometimes pulled her spine into a C.

On the night that Jennifer's breasts experienced their freedom, the awkward bra that contained them slipped its catch and pushed its hook into her skin. Jennifer wanted it fixed, though she couldn't make her mother understand. The confused woman adjusted the straps, discretely—reaching into Jennifer's collar so that the fighting men and boys would not see the act—and she told Jennifer to sit there and behave herself.

She turned and she left Jennifer alone for a short time. A little girl in a woman's body in a predicament, in a man's place in the world.

Jennifer's breasts were a bright white because they had never seen the sun. Aside from her hair, they were perhaps the only things about her that were normal. All of her other body parts had failed, to some degree, at their tasks. They did not see clearly. Or hear perfectly. Or walk with the proper amount of purpose. Nevertheless, Jennifer made do with those parts.

She accepted her full and round breasts, and their places at the front of her life, when they came upon her.

The truth is that Jennifer accepted her breasts much better than her mother did.

Jennifer's mother did not want the trappings of a woman's body to overtake her child. And Jennifer would always be a child. She would never have babies to nurse—or a lover to caress her.

She would not need breasts, her mother knew.

In Jennifer's life there had been very few men who truly understood her. Men, in general, avoided her because they could not make sense of her garbled speech and because her imperfections made them feel uncomfortable. They could not pat her on her twenty-year-old head, as they might a toddler's. And they could not admire her inner beauty, or confide in her as they did in old mothers, so they did nothing.

Her father did as well as any man could . . . and better than most.

Jennifer's fight with the bra began with a skirmish. She shrugged her shoulders and leaned forward and shrugged again. She shook through her skin like a horse does when it is trying to rid itself of flies.

Inside her shirt, her breasts rose and fell loosely. The catch swung freely, defiantly, until finally it seemed to Jennifer that she must take strong action.

She peeled her shirt over her head. And she peeled her bra. She flung the clothing aside; then she looked into her lap and she sat there, a naked C, and she waited—her breasts falling comfortably over a roll of fat and her folded arms.

There were boys and men in the room who somehow managed to cast their eyes away. No one spoke until the *dojo's* shocked master said to Jennifer's father, "Umm." And he gave her direction a nod.

Jennifer's father did as well as ever he had. Hurrying to cover her, he walked to the red line that separated the *dojo's* training ground from the common world, and he bowed properly, as he had been taught. He bowed to tradition and rules and ancient formalities. He bowed to his own surprise. And he bowed to simple bravery. But he did not know it.

An Ice Jacket Full of the Sun

Do you think life is adventure?

I push the button alongside the bright orange door of my mother's home and wait for my eighteen-year-old daughter to answer.

There was a time when this was my home too.

Standing on its front porch, listening to the door bell go through its familiar rings, I try to recall if there was ever a day in my life when my mother trusted me like she is trusting my daughter: alone in her house as she and my father vacation.

I think hard, but I can't even remember the last time I was in their home when they weren't there.

The solitude and the loneliness that accompany their absence make me mildly uncomfortable.

I chase away this unwanted thought, for which my mother is partly responsible: Someday I will have to come here knowing they won't be back.

Mother never leaves town that she does not bring to me her "everything-you'll-need-to-know-in-case-I-die" box. It is a compact, black, fireproof item that contains receipts, wills, insurance papers and banking information—the papers I'll need to get organized in the event that the unexpected happens.

There is a chill at my back, but I think about the box and laugh anyway.

I am confident of two things: With Mother the unexpected is always happening. And Death has definitely met his match.

Mother intends to wring every precious moment out of her life. She's had cancer. She's had a brain aneurysm. And even now she faces the possibility of open heart surgery for a condition called mitral valve prolapse.

She never discusses these illnesses that she does not shrug. In doing so, she is saying, "So?"

Mother will be seventy in April. And she still looks good. A trim figure. Full lips and creamy skin. Nicely styled, thick white hair. A quick and enthusiastic, if sometimes forgetful, mind.

She has always been a gadabout, taking my sister and me, as children, across the United States and then, after we'd married, traveling to one country after another, full of the curiosities and fascinations that accompany wanderlust.

The places she's been sound as if they absolutely brim with magic when she speaks of them: China. Brazil. Israel. Spain. Jerusalem. Ireland.

And the people!

She's been chased by a stranger in the Middle East, danced with Greeks in the Mediterranean and, oh! don't you know it gave her chills to walk where Jesus walked.

This time, Mother is contenting herself with a trip to Florida.

She's gone to visit two of her best friends, one from childhood and one from her middle age.

We almost lost Mother in 1976 when an aneurysm ruptured deep inside her brain.

She had been riding her stationary bicycle in the basement when the aneurysm went off like a bomb. Devastating but not deadly, it pushed unbearable pain through her head, but left her conscious.

Mother stumbled her way upstairs and went to bed, calling me from her bedside phone.

"I have a sick headache," she told me, not realizing the close call she had just experienced.

Sick headaches were nothing new. I had watched her suffer through them—migraines—for years.

I was twenty-five when Mother's cerebral aneurysm broke. I was a mother myself by that time, having given birth to the previously mentioned, much-trusted granddaughter. But I wasn't very experienced.

When Mother called me to tell me she was ill, I did all I knew to do. I went and sat at her bedside—hadn't she done this for me a hundred times?—and I took her some hot chicken soup.

We didn't think to call doctors until the aneurysm sounded a second alarm two days later.

They told us that she should undergo emergency surgery, but they tempered their advice with caution: Regardless of what they did or did not do, she might survive, she might die, or she might become a "vegetable."

There were no guarantees. And there are no words to describe the horror these possibilities presented to everyone but Mother.

She came to a decision easily, making the following remark: "Well, I can't just sit and twiddle my thumbs for the rest of my life."

She went for it, another adventure, flashing us the "OK" sign with her forefinger and thumb as orderlies wheeled her into the operating room.

How I cried.

Later, as she healed under a half-bald hairdo and a mass of white bandages, we feared the worst for her. She spoke in confused and twisted sentences, mentioning things only she could understand.

She requested, for example, "an ice jacket full of the sun."

That image, cold and ruthless as the invasion she had just been subjected to, yet full of brightness and hope, amazes me still.

I would have gotten her one at any price.

She settled for a drink of water.

Sometimes, when we get together these days, I ask her, "Where did the time go?"

I remark, amazed, that already my oldest daughter is a grown woman. What I'm really thinking is this: Already my mother is old.

130

It seems like only yesterday she was my age. Middle-aged. Teaching my sister and me life's greater and lesser lessons.

Consider this: John F. Kennedy has been killed. It is a gloomy and a sad day.

His funeral procession is making its way across our television set, its somber mood, its black and gray colors matching the rainy November weather outside our home.

"Stand up," Mother says to us, "the *National Anthem* is playing."

And so we stand, the three of us, silently saluting the television, paying a heartfelt tribute to our dead president from the remoteness of our living room.

Or this: "You girls don't know how to have fun."

Mother is several seconds into the General Motors employee picnic foot race, and she has put her shoe into the hem of her dress. She is sprawled full-length on her stomach, and she is grimacing in pain.

She is more than a little dusty. Holding her arm, she stands up and makes her way uphill to where my sister and I stand with our incredulous father.

There is a frenzied discussion, and Mother departs for the doctor.

Mother still wears the scar she received on her elbow that day. It was scraped to the bone, evidence of her peculiar victory. Life is a gamble, but it is for enjoying. And it comes with a price.

She wears a few other scars, too. One winds its way across her neck, a faded reminder of her thyroid operation.

Another (she won't show it to me) makes its way across her chest and under her arm. Her left breast is missing.

"You girls need to learn how to share," she tells my sister and me one Christmas season as she makes plans to bring an orphan into our home.

The girl comes, skinny and timid, and clings to our mother as only a lonely, hurting, desperate child would.

"Can I call you Mama?" she asks her eagerly, having just arrived at our home.

She follows my mother everywhere and even parks herself outside the bathroom door when necessary, waiting for my mother to emerge.

"Of course you can," Mother replies, and I am jealous.

It bothers her still that she wasn't able to keep the girl who, because of a troubled past, was deemed unadoptable at the time.

Over the course of my life, Mother has repeatedly made notice of those with less fortunate circumstances.

"There, but for the grace of God, go you," she's told me thousands of times.

And I have come to believe her.

She never pitches that phrase that she does not go on to tell me that she's had a full life.

"There's not much I've missed," she says, and she is right.

My daughter is glad for the opportunity to stay alone at my mother's house. She answers the ringing bell, finally (it's been ringing forever), and lets me into my mother's home with a broad grin on her face.

So this is what it's like to be independent?

My daughter, still getting her education and her bearings, can hardly wait to be on her own. Free from my ever-watchful eyes. Free to keep late hours. Spend her money. Make her own decisions.

I let her go a little at a time.

It's not easy, is it, Mom?

The Standard for Courage

What do butterflies feel like in your stomach?

When the surgeon came to talk with us after my mother's open heart surgery last week, he said her heart is far larger than it should be. This explains why a sensitive hand could feel it beating through her thin skin, way down by her side-waist, all of these past months.

I asked him, "Couldn't you tell that ahead of the surgery with the tests you performed?"

The truth is, though, that I was not entirely surprised by his comment. I have known my mother has a big heart since I was a child.

Over the years, she's had room in there for all sorts of things: Lost dogs, wild animals and strangers, lonely children and sons-in-law, foreigners, tricksters, musicians and weird relatives and on and on.

"There but for the grace of God . . . ." she used to say, regularly, while going energetically about her kitchen duties. And I believed her. Hers was a compassion taught by example. The problems of others, she meant, could just as easily have been our own.

When they became our own (has there ever been a life without problems?) my mother set the standard for courage. She hunkered down and took the necessary action.

In my youth, I watched while my mother—like so many mothers—played nurse, teacher and helpmate. I watched while she nursed our beloved dog back from a very close brush with death. And I watched her assist, ever-so-gently, at the delivery of kittens in our garage, too.

I watched while she chaperoned at girl scouting events. And while she drove to rock concerts.

In my youth, I watched while she taught (sometimes with white knuckles) the lessons of swimming and driving. While she demonstrated headstands and yoga. While she camped, partied or vacationed.

I watched while my mother laughed. And I watched one spring while she cared for her own dying mother.

I watched (though my mother did not know it) when she got

down on her knees at the side of my childhood bed and prayed.

I can see her still, through little slits between my supposedly sleeping eyelids, in the darkness of my bedroom: a vague and peaceful woman's image, a real presence with closed eyes and folded hands, whispering to God.

If ever anyone's life fell under God's grace, it was—and is—my mother's. She's survived cancer, a brain hemorrhage and now open heart surgery.

I am sitting in a quiet room as I write this. I cannot help but see my mother in a thousand different settings. She is dancing with my father. Driving me to band practice. Slipping me "mad money" to go on dates. Unloading my belongings in my dormitory room. Assisting me into my wedding gown. Helping me to decorate my firstborn's nursery. Helping only a short time later to select his burial clothes.

She is grinning through the baptisms of those among my children who survived.

I am picturing the two of us as we appeared in the hospital after her heart surgery, bound by blood and experience and the realities of motherhood.

My mother is asleep, still under the effects of anesthesia. Her face is swollen and contorted from her ordeal.

This time, I am the one to offer prayers at the side of a bed. I reach out and touch my mother's cool, white skin. For the first time, I genuinely see all of her seventy-seven years.

I speak to her sleeping form, blink away tears and send a plea toward heaven.

How do I know that God is listening? I know because my mother told me. Because she showed me. And that is all I need to know.

To The Perfectionist

Did you ever celebrate an anniversary of your first kiss?

We sometimes argue over the simplest things. I open the window an inch or so, eager to let in fresh air even though you, skinny, are shivering. A wind catches us and it is no surprise.

It is, after all, a Michigan winter.

Still, I do not want to miss the first wafts of spring air. And who knows, these days, when they will come? The seasons of Nature—and of our lives—do not seem as well-defined as they were when we were children.

Winter, especially, is not what it once was. Snows don't necessarily show themselves before Christmas. And they aren't necessarily deep and worth packing. And they don't necessarily linger until the last minute so that our snow forts have a good, long, fighting chance.

Do you remember how spring used to arrive, full of splendor each year? How it used to hang around, pleasantly? How it used to comfort us and offer hope?

Seems like it has, more recently, become all but a non-entity. It doesn't claim itself like it used to. Doesn't stop and appreciate its own beauty.

Spring reminds me of a mother on the run. Accepting a hand-off from winter, pausing only to catch its breath, and then hurrying directly into summer and its crowded hot days. The very buds of flowers hurry to catch up.

I caught the scents of spring early this year. On, if you can believe it, a February morning.

The scents slipped through the window we argue about. They awoke me from my sleep and tugged me out from under the covers so that I was happy on this particular morning to sit at the edge of the bed and just breathe.

With each breath I was a child again. My hair flowed down my back and trailed me like a kite tail. I wore my size eight, hooded, pink-plaid jacket. And I ran on legs that didn't throb from the effort.

Don't you wish we could go back to that time for just one day and be only friends? Maybe we could go fishing (you could do the worm). Maybe we could climb a tree and eat our lunches there, or play frozen tag, or pop those old-fashioned rolls of caps with stones. Or play flashlight tag.

Maybe we could flirt on the swing set at school.

What do you think it would be like to take our children with us? To actually befriend them? Do you think, then, they would understand that our childhoods were once real places? That there was a time when we were young? Less worried? Less consumed with regrets?

I would love, just once, to gather them about us—all of us equal in age—under the choke cherry tree and at the edge of the lawn, where we could draw a big circle in the adjoining sand, build tees out of dirt and shoot the few multi-colored marble shooters that have survived into my adulthood.

The first scents of spring have a power over me. There is something about those scents that is as familiar and welcome as your after-shave. They have a way of coaxing me.

I catch them when I can, even if it means risking an argument about opening the window while the furnace still runs.

"Let it run," is what I say.

It can run circles around us, and I promise you I will not care.

Mrs. X's Soul Mate Takes Flight

Mom, do you like bugs?

One night after what seemed like months of general chaos in her life, a tired Mrs. X found herself alone in her house. Grateful for the temporary solitude, she paused to consider the everyday sounds with which she had, over time, lost touch.

She noticed the quiet hum of her refrigerator. The gentle ticking of her stove clock. The drone of the distant furnace forcing warm air up through a nearby vent.

Mrs. X felt the air encircling her ankles and calves. It pushed over the stubby hairs that dotted her legs the way a wind pushes over nettles growing low to the ground. She reached down to rub one spot that tickled and then turned to open her kitchen window, facing a black sky and the halo of a distant streetlight.

Her fingers alighted on the frame's old metal handle, and she twisted it around, once, twice—opening the window just a fraction and letting in a blast of frigid November air.

As she did so, a single bug whooshed in.

It came from the dark of night into the soft glow of Mrs. X's kitchen and briefly stalled itself in mid-air. Mrs. X watched, surprised, while it flapped its wings furiously in an effort to gain control over its destiny.

Mrs. X even imagined that she heard the wind-blown bug go, "Whoa!"

Resisting an urge to swat at it, Mrs. X thought, "Drat! It's a renegade winter fly," and she put her hands on her hips in disgust as the bug expertly and efficiently pulled in its wings and let itself drift down onto Mrs. X's wooden cutting board.

The wings folded themselves against the bug's back and converted to a shell with a deep-red, fingernail-polish coating and several black polka dots.

No fly at all, the bug got its bearings on its legs and settled itself while Mrs. X said with whispered astonishment:

"Why, Ladybug, what are you doing out on this cold night?"

Mrs. X had a personal policy against hurting ladybugs and was glad she had resisted the swat. She had favored ladybugs over all other bug types ever since she was a child.

(Oh, certainly, lightning bugs had charmed her, as did the occasional "walking stick." And butterflies could evoke more than a passing pleasure. But it was ladybugs that truly captured her heart.)

Silly as it seemed, Mrs. X had never lost her girlhood compassion for their plight, as she remembered it from a children's rhyme.

Ladybug, Ladybug, fly away home. Your house is on fire and your children have gone.

The rhyme had given Mrs. X her first uncomfortable notions about loneliness.

She watched while the ladybug walked daintily along the edge of her flour-dusted cutting board, getting, Mrs. X imagined, little clumps of damp piecrust stuck against the undersides of her feet.

The cutting board sat precariously near the edge of the sink, and Mrs. X nudged it over gently, toward the cookie jar, to prevent the bug from taking an unexpected plunge.

Beside them, a simple, homemade pie baked in the oven. Mrs. X wondered if the ladybug was even the least bit tempted by its inviting scents.

Mrs. X had the thermostat set on low, allowing the pie to bake slowly. She knew her family would be hungry when they arrived home later.

For a moment, Mrs. X took her eyes off the ladybug and peeked into the oven to check on the pie's progress. She was relieved to see that its crust was turning a tempting, golden brown.

When she returned her gaze to the cutting board, Mrs. X saw that the ladybug was no longer there. Searching her kitchen with her eyes for one quick moment, she at last located the ladybug crawling up a cupboard door on her way back toward the window.

The narrow slit Mrs. X had first created by opening the window remained, and she supposed that the ladybug would soon resume her flight.

Ladybug, Ladybug, fly away home . . . , Mrs. X sang to her little visitor, and she cranked the window a fraction wider to make the leaving easier.

Ladybug, Ladybug, fly away home . . . , she sang again, this time in a muted, respectful voice. Behind her, the humming refrigerator and the ticking clock and the droning furnace kept time.

About the Author

Carolyn Walker is an award-winning journalist. Her journalism work has appeared in *Detroit Monthly Magazine;* the *Detroit Free Press; Michigan; The Magazine of the Detroit News;* the *Flint Journal;* the *Observer & Eccentric* newspapers; the *Oakland Press* and the *Clarkston News.* She is a contributing writer of fiction, poetry and essays in the anthology *At the Edge of Mirror Lake.*

Walker has won first-place awards for her column writing from the Suburban Newspapers of America, the Michigan Press Association and the ARC/Oakland County.

A graduate of Oakland University, Walker is married and the mother of three. She is currently at work on a novel to be called *Solomon's Rock.*